# Friendly Enemies

*Is it ever ok to sleep with your best friend's girl?*

## Torrian Ferguson

www.anexanderbooks.com

TM

P.O. Box 3582
Greensboro, NC 27402
www.anexanderbooks.com

First printing November 2008

Printed in the United States of America

10 9 8 7 6 5 4 3 2 1

ISBN 978-0615220147

# Anexander Books Support Team

Editor: Chalonda Ferguson

Cover photographer:
 Arthur Rogers
 Artsho Creative Services
Arthur@artsho1.com


Cover Design:
K & D Creations
Marketing and Promotions:
Ferguson Literary Group


Literary Consultant:
Renaissance Management Services
Lisa Gibson
 www.renmanserv.com


www.anexanderbooks.com

# Acknowledgments

I would first like to thank my wife, Chalonda Ferguson, for staying by my side as I start a new chapter of my life. You've stuck with me during some of my best and worst ideas. You are my biggest fan and I love and cherish you every day for you being you.

Secondly, I would like to thank my family in Miami, Fl and Greensboro, NC for again standing by me. See mama, I'm getting better; this one's not as nasty.

Lisa Gibson, you are the reason I'm still in this industry. I've learned so much from you and I can never thank you enough for being not only my mentor but also my friend.

I also have to thank the ladies of OOSA Online Book Club. You all have no idea how much you really mean to me. Ms. Toni and Crystal, you two are the best friends any author can have. I'm lucky to know both of you.

Brian W. Smith. Thank you for giving me the blue print to do what I love to do. You are a friend for life.

Special thanks go out to the following:
Artist First Online Radio, N'tyse, Kesha Redmon, Deilra Smith-Collard, Shannon Davis, Marc Lacy, King Pen, James Muhammad, Kwabena Hobbs, ARC Online Book Club, APOO Book Club, Bronx Bookman, Kaira Denee, Hood Book Head Quarters, Vanessa Calvin, Richard and Connie Cheek, Martell Brown, Lloyd Rolle,

Teria Russell, Dwan McClain, Ursula Ivory, Dana Pitman, Miss Kris & Lady J of Can We Talk Radio, Stacie Brister and The Cleveland Public Library, Ruby Clark and family, Yolonda Battle, and every author I've ever had the pleasure of meeting. You all are wonderful people and I wish you the best in everything that you wish to do.

Thanks,

"An insincere and evil friend is more to be feared than a wild beast; a wild beast may wound your body, but an evil friend will wound your mind."

~Buddha

# Chapter 1...First Impressions

Women will make you do some stupid shit, but pussy will make you lose your damn mind. Getting on that damn chat line was a blessing and a curse. That's all I could think about as I lay here looking up into the lights. It's funny, I'm at peace right now, but I thought it would be different. But, I guess this is the perfect time for me to reflect on all the decisions I've made over the last year.

*****************************************

"Jay, I said call me when your bus get here and I'll pick you up. Damn stop trippin'".

"Jay is my best friend, but damn he get on my nerves," I said to myself, as I hung up the phone. Part of me is excited to see my friend, but part of me is still pissed off at what he did a few months back while I was still living in Miami.

"Niggas always worried 'bout some shit," I said to myself, as I stood in the mirror getting ready to go to work. A few seconds later, a smile danced across my face as I washed up and thought about the sex I was gonna have with Tracy.

Being new in town and not knowing a soul here, watching TV got old, real fast. Not to mention, I was starting to get horny as hell. I had to do something to get back to myself; "The Playa of Playas".

Tracy was a college senior that I had met on the local telephone chat line. Tonight after work, I was going to meet her for the first time at her on-campus apartment.

While shaving my head in the mirror, I started to think about all the different positions I was going to fuck her in.

"I'm gonna ride that ass doggy style, flip her on her back, press her knees into her chest and beat the hair off that pussy," I said to myself, as I repeatedly rubbed the top of my head, making sure there were no missed spots of hair still there.

When I finished shaving, I took a long look at myself to make sure everything was tight. I had to make sure that the best looking man in North Carolina was perfect. Being a dark skinned brotha, I had to keep the lotion in my pocket, just in case the skin got a little dry. I can't go around talking to the ladies all ashy. The goatee was tight and my face was smooth. As I stood there looking at this 6'3, 230 lb solid built frame, I knew tonight would be a special night with Tracy. This was my first date since moving to North Carolina two months ago, and it was time to get out and see what Greensboro women had to offer.

Since moving here, I found a job working as a chef in a fancy downtown hotel restaurant. The menu consists of Filet Mignon, Herb Crust Salmon, and Pan Seared Sea Bass. If you were looking for something to eat under $50.00 a plate, you were in the wrong spot. Hell, our appetizers cost $15.00 or better.

Tonight of all nights, we would be busy as hell. I thought I could go in and work an easy shift, hit the clock, then hit some ass. But I guess I was the only one in the city that had plans. It seemed like everybody in town was in the restaurant tonight eating a five course meal. I was tired as all get out, but I instantly perked up when I heard the Executive Chef say,

"20 minutes till closing!"

That was all I needed to hear. I put it into another gear and started banging out orders; trying to hurry up so I could get out of there and make it to my date on time.

"What you in such a rush for tonight?" my co-worker Allen asked; as I quickly cleaned off the spot he had been working all night.

"I met this girl on the chat-line the other night and she sounds like she is fine as hell," I said, while tossing dirty pots and pans on a cart and running them to the dish room.

"Chat line?" he asked, looking at me like I was saying something in Latin.

"Yeah, that new party line on the phone. I was watching TV the other night, when this commercial came on talking about meet new friends from all over the state. I gave it a call and got 90 minutes free to talk to all the women I want." He was now looking at me like I was lying through my teeth. "You have to give your age, describe yourself and what you are looking for, sit back, then let them hit you up if they are interested."

Allen now had that look of tell me more on his face. He stopped working and hung on every word I was saying.

"Man, she said she was 5'5, light skinned with a short classy haircut, and fills out a pair of jeans nicely."

"Thick in all the right places huh?"

I nodded my head yes and smiled from ear to ear.

"That means she's fat!" he said, laughing hysterically in my face.

I quickly replied, "thick, fat, chunky, fluffy I don't give a damn, all I know is, that ass is mine tonight."

Walking around like king of the jungle, I continued, "her ad said she is looking for casual friends and someone to spend a little time with here and there. You know like I know, that means; she wants a fuck buddy."

After I told Allen that, he looked sick and constipated. He knew within the hour I was going to be balls deep in some pussy, and he was going to be alone with a porno wishing he were me.

The rest of the shift, Allen talked about the chat line. After a while, he got on my damn nerves talking about it. The more he talked the slower he cleaned, which meant the longer it would be before I got the hell out of the restaurant.

After showering and changing at work, I drove over to Tracy's apartment. I had never been on that side of town before, so I had no clue where I was going. But one thing is always the same, no matter what city you go to. The projects are the projects. Some may be tall buildings, others might be flats, but the smell of the air is the same. That unmistakable tan and brown paint on the buildings is always another dead giveaway. I found the apartment I was supposed to be going to, got out of my car and made sure my damn alarm was on. I was not use to the projects, but I had always heard the best pussy is in the hood, so I figured what the fuck, go lay it down and get the hell out of there. I had no intentions on staying around afterwards and talking or cuddling. Give me the ass and let me go. Evidently, Tracy was peeking out the closed window shades as I walked up, because before I could knock on the door, she opened it.

Stunned at the door suddenly opening, I stepped back and drew back my fist, ready to throw the first punch. You got to stay on your guard around here. Muthafuckas seem to jump out of walls in the projects. And they always know your ass don't belong there.

As the door opened, I couldn't help but stand there and look at the biggest damn breast I'd ever seen, spilling out the top of a half buttoned red blouse.

"Hi I'm Tracy, come on in."

I wanted to dive face first into her chest, but you know I had to play it cool.

"How you doing? I'm Gerald," I said, trying not to look at Tracy's breast as they made their own introduction. She walked away from the door and I walked in the front room behind her. My eyes were instantly fixed on her big round apple shaped behind stuffed into those tiny Hilfiger Jeans. She had to have jumped off the bed into those jeans. They were tight as hell and showed me what I was in store for in a few minutes. As we sat down on her sofa, I could not help but notice all the pictures on the wall. They were all hot spots in New Orleans.

"Have a thing for New Orleans, huh?" I asked looking around the room.

"Of course, that's home for me. I moved here about a year ago."

"I've been there a few times myself. Hung out in the French Quarters a time or two, but home for me is Miami," her eyes widened a bit when she heard that.

"What the hell are you doing here then? Miami is off the chain, from what I hear."

I started telling her about Bayside Shops, which is a very upscale and trendy shopping expo right on the water of Biscayne Bay. I told her about Cocoa Walk, another very trendy nightspot in Coconut Grove. She seemed very interested in every word that came out my mouth.

Just so it did not seem I was only interested with talking about Miami, I asked, "So what is it that you are looking for on the chat-line?"

"To be honest I'm looking for a guy to break me off every now and then, nothing serious, I have a man at home."

That's exactly what I wanted to hear. I was not looking for a relationship. I was just on a mission to fuck as much as possible. Besides I just had a breakup back home and was not ready to settle with any one particular person.

"That's cool with me; I'm looking for the same thing."

With that, it was kinda an uncomfortable silence between us. I could tell we were both wondering who was going to be the one to get it on and popping.

I figured, fuck it I'll say something and see where it goes.

"So, is it possible that I can be that casual friend you are talking about?"

Tracy looked at me, smiled, and answered, "Sure, not a problem at all, as long as there is no baby mama drama in my parking lot. I'm down for whateva."

I put my hand on her thigh and rubbed, as we did that soap opera stare at each other. Evidently, I was moving to slow for her. She stood up, straddled me, and shoved her tongue into my mouth. I was a little shocked, but I shook that off quick when I felt my dick start to let me know it's was just about time for him to make his debut to the party. My large hands were all over her butt in those tight jeans. My manhood was getting harder and harder by the second. She started kissing me on my neck; licking from my neck to my ears. As she did this, I moaned just a little to let her know that I was really feeling her.

I reached under the back of her shirt and rubber her soft high yella skin. I slid my hands into the back of her jeans. She was wearing a thong, and that drove me over the edge. She had her hands under my shirt rubbing my hairy chest and pinching my nipples. I undid the buttons on her shirt and raised her red lace bra from the bottom so that her round beautiful breasts could fall from the cups. While sucking on her right nipple, I gently squeezed the left one. Every so often, I would flick my tongue over her nipple, just teasing it before sucking on it again. She began to moan softly as I kissed and sucked on her breasts and neck.

She took off my shirt and asked me to stand up. She ran her hands around my dick that was desperately trying to get out of my jeans. She unbuckled my belt and unzipped my pants. I was wearing a pair of black boxer briefs and a hard dick. She grabbed my manhood, which by now was hard enough to cut a diamond, and stroked it a few times. My erection was 9 inches long and as thick as a baby bottle. She licked along every vein in it before taking me into her mouth.

Damn, she's the bomb, I thought as she sucked hard and fast on my erection. She used a lot of spit, and that was right up my alley. I like women who are not afraid to get sloppy with it; slobbering on the dick and letting that spit run off the chin.

I grabbed the back of her head and let her do her thing for another ten minutes. When I felt myself about to cum, I stopped her

"I want to taste you," I said to her and she was more than happy to let me taste all I wanted.

I unbuttoned her jeans and laid her on the floor with nothing but her thong on. I slid between her legs with my face inches away from her slit. I stuck out my tongue and licked the fabric covering her pussy. The scent of her vagina was enough to make any man want to have sex. I pulled the thongs to the side.

"Damn, you have a pretty pussy," I said to her, looking almost amazed.

"And it's wet too" she answered, taking one of her fingers and putting it in to show just how wet and sticky she was. I sucked on her cum covered finger, and then began to eat her out.

Every time I would suck on her clit, she would arch her back and moan loud as hell.

"Eat this pussy nigga!" she yelled, getting into it more and more by the second. I like a woman that talks a little shit while getting hers. That's a huge turn on to me. She grabbed my baldhead and pulled me further into her pussy. When I started short sucking her clit that was all she wrote. She began to wiggle around on the floor while holding my head between her legs.

"Right there, right there shit that's what I'm talkin' bout. Eat this pussy, eat It." she demanded. I must have hit that spot because she squirted her sweet juices down my throat, with some spilling down out onto my chin. I was so turned on by her vulgar words that I licked every drop of cum she had.

When I was finished eating her, I quickly turned her over in the doggy style position. I grabbed a condom out of my pants pocket, lying in a pile next to us. I slammed into her fat pussy repeatedly, trying to break her back with my thrusts. The harder I hit it, the more vulgar she talked to me.

"Harder, harder beat this pussy" the more she talked the harder I pounded into her. I turned her over again and got on top, putting her in the buck position. Her legs were on my shoulders and I was pounding right into her. There was nothing between us but 9 inches of hard dick, and I was using it to kill her pussy. I drilled into her like an Arab looking for oil.

"You like this dick don't you?" All she could do was cry out in pure ecstasy.

While in this position, I could suck her breast every so often and that drove her wild. After about fifteen minutes, I felt myself about to let loose.

"I'm 'bout to cum. Where you want it?"

"On my titties baby."

Just then, I pulled out snatched, the condom off and sprayed her large breasts with warm semen.

"Yeah baby, shoot that cum for me," she begged. I stroked my dick for every last drop.

We got up and sat on the couch. "So?" she asked.

"So what?"

"How was it?"

With a wide grin on my face, I said, "It was the bomb". She smiled and began looking for her clothes. After getting dressed, she walked me to the door.

"I'll call you aiight," I said, as I walked past her going out the door.

She kinda looked like, what the hell?

"Do not call me. I'll call you when I need you."

I was like, what the fuck just happened, but I had to play it off.

"That cool," I said, walking away.

While driving home, I burst out laughing

"She fucked me and let me go. Ain't that some shit?"

When I got home, I thought, who else is on the line tonight that might want to get up. After a long shower, I picked up the phone and called the line. "87 women on line," the automated voice said, "Your free membership is up. You can purchase more time with a credit card." As I scrambled for my wallet to get my Visa, it never crossed my mind the dangerous world I was entering.

The morning after being dismissed by Tracy, I woke up knowing that my best friend was coming into town for a short visit. Half of me was excited to see my friend the other half still was a little uneasy around him. I drove to the Bus Depot on Washington Street and saw him standing outside looking like a lost child. His eyes were as wide as saucers and he looked as if someone had dropped him off on the side of a country road. When I first moved to Greensboro, it took a while to get use to things here. One thing I still have not gotten use to is a stranger just walking past you and saying hello. Back in Miami you didn't speak to anybody unless you knew them. You really didn't acknowledge the person next to you. Shit, if you did, they were going to look at you like you had lost your damn mind. What the hell are you talking to me for, written all over their face. And if you spoke to one of those snooty ghetto women you, just might get your ass cursed out. So coming here and having someone just simply ask how you're doing, was culture shock for me; and he looked like someone had just made that mistake with him. I pulled the car up to where he was standing and got out.

"Wuz up dawg? How was your trip?" I asked, as I walked up to Jay, giving him some dap and a one armed hug. Jay was a light skinned brother with wavy hair, 6'2, and 260lbs, always dressed in the latest gear, and looking for the women.

"It was aiight. Just tired as hell from that long ass trip. I'll never catch the bus from Florida to North Carolina again."

I noticed Jay was standing there with about two large suitcases and three duffel bags of clothes with him. That was a lot of shit for a person that originally told me they were just coming to hang out for about a week or so.

"How long you staying again?" I asked, as I helped him heave one of those heavy ass bags into my trunk.

"I just decided to stay up here for a while. You know, till I get things together."

"You staying?" he could see the, oh hell no look all over my face.

"Yeah, I figured you wouldn't mind if your boy came and kicked it with you for a while."

The truth is, I did mind. I was just getting use to having my place to myself. If it was something on the floor, I put it there. If there was no milk in the refrigerator, I drank the last of it. Now I'm back to wondering who touched my shit, who feet stanking up the house? I'm back to that roommate shit again. Nevertheless, that was my boy so I tried not to show how pissed off I was at his ass acting all niggerish and not having the common courtesy to let me know what his true plans were.

"So where them hoes at man?" Jay asked, as we drove past North Carolina A&M University. I will say this about N. C. A&M, they are known for having the finest women in the Carolinas attending that school. I know every college has fine women but it was something about those A & M women that made them stand out.

"On the phone." I looked out the corner of my eye and could tell Jay had no clue what the hell I was talking about. He started looking around to see if there was a fine ass woman outside using her phone.

"What the hell do you mean, on the phone?"

We pulled into my apartment complex and he was still looking around for that fine ass female that was on the phone.

"Come in the house and I'll show you what I'm talking about."

After unloading all of Jay's things, he sat down on the sofa and I sat in the big lazy boy recliner. The question was asked again.

"So tell me about the women on the phone, nigga," Jay asked again, sounding more interested than the first time he had asked. I couldn't do anything but laugh at the eagerness that was in his voice.

"It's a party line you call to hook up with women looking for the same things you are."

"Sounds like some phone sex type shit to me," Jay said, laughing a little.

"Nah, it ain't like that. These are everyday women in the area that wants to get theirs. Some want long term relationships, while others want a one night stand. Anything you are into is on that line, trust me." I sounded like a used car salesman trying to sell a lemon, but Jay was sold on it.

The two of us were know in college for tag teaming women at our apartment. One would have his way with a woman then let his boy come in and do the same. We both had a way of talking women into almost anything we wanted them to do.

"How do I get on this party line?" Jay asked, ready to see if it was as easy as I had made it sound. I gave him the number, and Jay's eyes lit up like a faggot that just got a huge bag of dicks on Christmas morning. I thought he was going to chill for a moment or at least try to tell me how things were back home, after I left the way I did. His ass reached for the phone and started dialing. I turned on the TV and tried not to listen to him as he set up his password, got his membership number, and free 90 minutes. The system requested Jay to record a message describing what he was looking for in a woman. The way the system was set up, you would record a message for women to listen to. If they liked what they heard, they would leave you a message telling you they want to talk. You could message back and forth to feel each other out or you could just jump into a live conversation with the person on the spot. Kinda like instant messenger, but on the phone.

"What's goin' on ladies? My name is Jay and I'm new to the area," he said, in a low deep voice sounding like a fake ass Barry White.

"I'm a 6'2, 260 lb, light-skinned college graduate, looking for a full figured, voluptuous sistah to spend a little time with. I am not looking for anything long-term, just someone to hang out and chill with. So if this is you, please hit me up."

As soon as Jay stopped recording, I burst out laughing so hard, I fell out of my chair.

"Full figured! What the hell is that about?"

"Shit nigga, big girls need love to and believe it or not, they don't come with all the hang ups those skinny ass women do. Big girls just want to get their freak on and let that be that. None of that come bond with me shit."

We were both laughing at this point. I thought back to Tracy. She was a thick girl. She was every bit 170 -180 lbs. I guess that could pass for full figured in the eyes of most and she was a freak too. He might have a point, I thought to myself.

Jay sat there for about two minutes, and then the automated voice spoke to him, "You have a message. To hear it, press 1."

Jay damn near jumped out the chair when he heard the voice. He was just sitting there listening to the women's recordings saying what they were looking for on the line.

"I gotta message dawg!" he said, sounding as excited.

Jay pressed 1 and listened to his first message. A smile ran across his face very quick as he listened.

"I heard your ad and I think I fit the profile you are looking for. My name is Destiny. If you want to learn more about me, let's talk and see what happens."

Her voice was smooth as silk. She did not sound ghetto and she talked like she had some sense.

"Playa, what do I do. She wants to talk." Jay asked sounding almost frantic

"Send her a message back. Ask her what she's trying to get into tonight. You don't want to waste all your free time talking to one woman; when there's a dozen more wanting to talk."

Jay sat and prepared himself to send a message. He cleared his throat, so I knew he was getting ready to go into "Barry White" mode.

"Hello, Destiny. I got your message and you sound like a woman I would like to get to know better. If you want, leave me your number so I can call you a little later."

After he sent Destiny her message back, he received another message. "Hello my name is Angela and I'm new to the area also. I'm full figured with a caramel complexion, and long black hair. I'm twenty-five; don't have kids, and own my own place. If you are interested hit me back."

Jay was in total shock. He could not believe that it was this easy to meet women this way. He was like a kid in a candy store, smiling and laughing the entire time.

"I got your message Angela, and I would love to get to know you a little better. Describe yourself in detail for me and we'll take it from there."

Destiny also hit Jay back with a message. "Here is my number, 336-555-9876. I have to get off the line in a minute, so feel free to call me tonight after 8:00, bye."

Jay was stomping his feet and punching the air. He looked over at me sitting in the recliner, trying to ignore him.

"I've been in town for all of an hour and already pulling women. I'm the shit, nigga!" he said, smiling from ear to ear, feeling proud of himself and nodding his head to a beat that only he could hear.

"Just like old times, huh?" I asked, as I walked out the room to shower for work.

"Hell yeah! I'm loving this shit," Jay replied, as he continued to listen to ads and leave messages for women.

Jay had his pick of women on the line. There were woman on the line from all walks of life. You had the ghetto chicks that liked to leave messages you could hardly make out what they were saying. "Hey boo, this be your girl, Lil Mama A.K.A. Lil Red, and I wanna know what you trying to get into. You know what I be sayin'? I'm down for whateva. You know what I'm sayin'? I know you tryin' to get yours and I'm doin' the same, so hit me back. You feelin me? Holla at cha girl."

Then, you had the women that just hated on the fact that a man was on the line looking for only full figured women. "I heard your message and you know what? That's jacked up that you only want fat girls. You must be fat yourself! Some people on here don't care what a person look like but obviously you are not one of those open-minded people. I hate people like you! Only full figured women; what's wrong with us skinny women? You must have something wrong with you if you like to have all that fat just jiggling round when you fuck; nasty, fat muthafucka!"

But the one that caught both our attention were the ones that sounded like they had a little sense in her head. "Hello, I'm a full figured African American female. I'm Looking for a nice guy that want to get together for a few drinks and have a good time. I'm very top heavy and sexy as they come. I'm also disease and drug free and you need to be the same. I don't care if you have a woman because I have a man. I'm just trying to meet new friends. If this sound interesting to you, please leave me a message, bye."

I was all the way into the bedroom and heard Jay yell, "I'm never leaving Greensboro. This is pussy paradise."

I thought to myself, what the fuck have I done?

A few months have passed and my attitude is getting funkier and funkier by the day. One thing I cannot stand is a grown ass man not working. If I'm able to get up and go to work; I know Jay's big able ass can get up and at least try to find a job. Shit, he's made it obvious he's not going anywhere, so the least he could do is get a job and try to help out with the bills since; he's sucking up all the cool air and drinking up all the juice and soda. That nigga even ate my last Strawberry Pop Tart and put the empty box back in the cabinet. How you eat another nigga's Pop Tart? That was the last damn straw. As I slammed the empty box into the over flowing trashcan, Jay walked around the corner and had the nerve to open cabinets looking for something else to eat. I lit into his ass.

"Dawg you gotta get a job," I said, sounding more like Jay's father than his best friend. "You've been here for three months and I thought you were staying for a little while You know, a couple of months to get on your feet."

If looks could kill he would have been a dead mutha-fucka because I was staring a second hole into his ass. My mom always said when I get angry I look just like my father. My eyes bulge out a little and I get two shades darker. I must have looked like midnight during a power outage, cause I was mad as hell. Jay just stood there looking like a lost child. He never even made an attempt to say anything. So, I just kept going. I figured why stop now, hell I'm on a roll.

"Since I see that you are not going anywhere, anytime soon, you have to get a gig." Jay tried to act like he wasn't paying me much attention, but he heard every word I was saying.

After a few seconds of me standing directly in front of him staring, telling him how I felt and what he was going to do, Jay finally spoke up.

"Aiight man, I'll look for one today!" he snapped, with a very irritated look on his face. The two of us were friends, but that best friend shit, was fading and fading fast. I be damned if I was going to pay another month for a grown man to live for free. I couldn't live with myself if I knew I was living with someone and not carrying my weight. Jay had no problem with it at all. But since it was my apartment, my rules went and he knew I meant every word I said. He also knew not to push my limits.

Some of my anger might be because of the shit that went down back in Miami. As a matter of fact, I know 50% of my anger is because of that.

While in college, Jay and I were the best of friends until Jay let me walk into a life-altering situation with an ex-girlfriend, and that was unforgivable to me. I admit, I am always a little bossy to Jay. He just always sit there and take it. I knew I could get away with talking to Jay any kinda way and he would do nothing about it. Jay was a very laid-back ladies man. The only time he ever got excited and got loud was when women were involved. I, on the other hand, was very loud, strong willed and told you what I was and was not going to do. Taking lip from someone has never been a talent of mine.

After a couple of days, Jay's new friend, Destiny, helped him find a job. The new problem now was that I had to take his ass to work and pick him up. I'm the type that doesn't mind helping a person out every now and then, but taking Jay to work and picking him up every day was getting old very fast. To make matters worse, he was not coming out of the building on time. Each night he came out later and later. I knew as soon as he stepped foot in the car tonight I was going to tell his ass he had to find another way to work. But of course, he was late coming out, so telling him off had to wait as well. I had a few moments so I figured I'd call the line again to see what was poppin'.

"There are 130 women online," the automated voice said.

This of course was music to my ears. In the few months of me being in North Carolina, I've had to have slept with over 15 different women from this line. I felt like I had the biggest dick in the room every time I called.

I wonder who it'll be tonight, I thought to myself as I listened to each and every woman's ad, I had been with Janet the Flight Attendant; Rita the big boned Latina; and April a 6th year college senior who loved to fuck. These were just a few of the women I slept with, and never spoke to again. Little did I know, this night would be different.

"Hi, my name is Nicole. I heard your ad and you sound very interesting. I'm 5'8, mocha complexion, 44dd breast and I wear a size 18 in jeans so if you are interested hit me back. Peace."

I knew this was gonna be another hit and run as I like to call it. Hit the pussy and run out the door. I smiled from ear to ear as I got myself together to answer her message.

Looking at the phone, smiling, I started talking and motivating myself.

"That's the type of girl I'm talkin bout. Thick as hell with some big ass titties". Nicole sounded fine and I knew I was going to beat that pussy up. I sent her a message back.

"Hey this is Gerald and I really want to get up with you. If you want let's talk for a while and maybe get up later tonight."

It took about 3 minutes before Nicole messaged back.

"Hey, wuz up? I really want to meet you as well. But I'm going to be honest; I'm not one for beating around the bush. I'm horny as hell tonight. Do you think you can help me out?"

You would think that in today's society, people would be a little more careful about who they hang out with; let alone sleep with. I could be crazy as hell. I could be running around fucking bitches and cutting their heads off. Being a dude, I really don't have to worry about that kind of shit cause I'll dot a bitch's eye if she starts some funny shit. But, the women on the line for some reason really didn't care they wanted what they wanted and I was more than happy to give it to them.

After hearing Nicole's message I shook with excitement. I pressed all sorts of numbers trying to find the correct one to send her another message.

"Let's exchange numbers and give me your address and I'll be over there in an hour, aiight? Bye."

As I was writing down Nicole's address, Jay walked up and got into the car.

"Dawg, I'm really feeling my girl Destiny," I just looked at Jay as if the worst smell in the world was right under my nose.

"You calling that hoe from your job?" I asked still looking at Jay with the mean mug.

"Yeah we talked a few time today actually. It seems like all I do is think about her. I love the conversations that we have."

I burst out laughing, "Damn man she got YOU sound-ing like the bitch! You sure she ain't bending you over?"

Seeing Jay happy was something that I just couldn't take. Every opportunity I had to make Jay feel bad about himself or something he was doing, I took it. He needed to feel bad for the shit he did to me.

"Oh, by the way, I know you all in love now, but you got to tell your girl ease up on the phone a bit. Y'all on the phone all damn night and that shit is starting to get on my damn nerves. I'm still paying the bill, since you haven't got a dime to your name yet; and I can't even get on my fucking phone. I'm not about to use up my minutes on my cell either. So either you start paying for half the bill or talk at the job and don't touch my phone."

Jay looked like he wanted to jump up and say some-thing. But he knew that he was living in my house and I had no problem putting his ass out. So he just bit his tongue and listened as I went on.

"Don't get me wrong, I'm not saying you can't have phone calls but when the phone rings at 2 a.m., it pisses me off being awaken by some silly ass female looking to get used for a booty call."

Jay's ears turned bright red and he looked as if cursing me out was on the tip of his tongue. But again, he turned his head and looked out the car window.

"Whateva man. I'll just tell her not to call so late."

"I appreciate that man, I really do. But the next bitch you meet on the line, make sure she has a little home training. Most people know you don't call somebody house after 10pm, unless it's an emergency."

Jay just shook his head and looked out the window as we drove down the street. I smirked a little as we drove. I knew I had gotten under Jay's skin and that's exactly where I wanted to be.

A few minutes passed and I couldn't help starting up again about Destiny.

"How are you feeling Destiny, when you fuck more hoes than I do off the line?"

"That might be true, but she's the only one I'm still fucking."

If that shit made sense to him, then fuck it, it made sense to me. I didn't say another word for the rest of the trip home.

*************************************************

All of a sudden I felt a hand touch my face. I was looking directly at my girl and she was moving her mouth but I couldn't hear a word she was saying. I could tell people were running around next to me because I could feel the vibration of their feet hitting the pavement as I laid on the ground. She was the most beautiful woman I'd ever laid eyes on. I wanted to grab her and hold her close to me. I wanted to smell her favorite body spray, Japanese Cherry Blossom. But again for some reason I couldn't smell anything either. What the hell is going on with me? With everything that's going on, my mind slipped back into time and I recalled a conversation that my boy told me he had. But the funny thing was it was like I was in the room but they could not see or hear me.

\*\*\*\*\*\*\*\*\*\*\*\*\*\*\*\*\*\*\*\*\*\*\*\*\*\*\*\*\*\*\*\*\*\*\*\*\*\*\*\*\*\*\*\*\*\*\*\*

"Check this out. Gerald was tripping again today. He said that you are calling the house too much and to ease up a bit." I didn't even look up at her as I said that. I knew her face was all screwed up.

"Fuck him! Who the hell is he suppose to be!"

Destiny was a nice girl, but get her wrong and it was hell to pay. She too had a shape to die for and a good attitude but Gerald has rubbed her the wrong way since day one.

"I should go around there and whip his punk ass."

She didn't have a problem speaking her mind.

"Stop tripping baby. No need for all that. You know how he is and he's not gonna change. So fuck him."

"Why do you put up with his shit Jay?"

Destiny said still fuming mad at what I had just told her. I really didn't want to get into it. She didn't know and she had no reason to know so I tried my best to change the topic. I leaned over and grabbed her hand and tried to lead her to the bedroom.

"I know you ain't trying to get some tonight after your BOY told you to come over here and tell me to stop calling so much and you did it."

\*\*\*\*\*\*\*\*\*\*\*\*\*\*\*\*\*\*\*\*\*\*\*\*\*\*\*\*\*\*\*\*\*\*\*\*\*\*\*\*\*\*\*\*\*\*\*\*

On the way to Nicole's house my cell phone rang.

"Hello"

"Where you at?" A loud female voice screamed from the phone.

"You suppose to have been here 10 minutes ago."

I looked at the phone like, what the fuck?

"Who the fuck is this?" I asked, screaming back into the phone.

"This Nicole! You getting your women mixed up tonight?"

Right then, something in my head told me to turn around and go the fuck home. But my dick was telling me to hit it and be gone afterwards. The phone went silent for a few seconds.

"I'm pulling up now! Damn, chill out it's all good."

I hung up the phone and a sharp pain hit me in the stomach. I leaned over the steering wheel. As fast as the pain had hit me, it left. Again my mind told me to leave and again my dick pulled me in the other direction. As for the sharp pain in my stomach, I just passed it off as nerves.

I walked up to the door and could smell the fragrance of incense coming from under the door. I thought to myself, I wonder how many of those musk scent things she got lit up in there? I knocked on the door and stood back blowing my breath into my hand making sure I was straight. The door flung open

"Thought you were trying to play games and not show up!" I jumped back a little as this thick, light skin vixen stood talking to me.

"I told you I would be here."

I walked in and the first thing I noticed was a damn gold spider lamp standing in the corner. If it was one thing I hated, it was those damn spider lamps. And to make matters worse, two of the eight bulbs were burnt out. Nicole walked over to a C. D. player that was sitting on top of a couple of triple stacked milk crates with a table cloth over them and turned on that new Usher and Beyonce, In the Club remix. She then handed me a wine glass of her favorite Magnum 20/20, Banana Red.

After a few minutes of small talk, things quickly escalated.

"So how big is your dick?" I almost choked on my drink.

"A little forward aren't you?" I said, wiping my lips and pretending I didn't see that big ass German roach walking on the wall across the room.

"No need in beaten round the bush," she answered.

"Instead of me telling you, come over here and feel it and tell me how big you think it is."

Nicole walked over and placed a firm grip on my dick.

"I guess this will do for the night," she said, with a smirk. We went into her bedroom, which had the scent of Lysol, better yet, Lemon Fresh Lysol.

She began stripping for me. I was almost naked by the time she had taken off her pants.

"Damn nigga, you want this ass huh?" she commented, as I stood there in my boxer briefs.

"Bring that ass here," I said, as I stood next to the bed motioning for her to come over to me.

There was no romance involved. She wanted to fuck and that was all she wanted to do. She had on a pair of red see-thru bikinis that hugged her butt like they were her natural skin. I bent her over the bed, moved her panties to the side, and began to eat her out from the back. She rubbed her ass in my face, moaning louder every time she felt my tongue on her ass. I squeezed her butt cheeks with delight as I performed on her. I even smacked her on the butt a few times, to get the excitement level up. In one swift motion, I turned her over and was bringing my now hard member to her face. Before she could say a word, I was pushing my erection into her mouth. She began to gag a bit as she tried to deep throat me. She let me fall out of her mouth so she could suck on my balls. With every hum of her throat, excitement grew from my toes to the top of my head. I looked down and saw that she had her eyes closed and enjoying pleasing me. I smiled and even laughed a time or two to myself thinking, I just met this damn girl and she got my balls all in her mouth. The sad part is I didn't even take a bath before I came over here. She's just sucking my sweaty, funky ass balls.

Sensing I was about to cum she gave me a condom.

"Fuck this pussy," she demanded.

I put the condom on and began to pound her for all she was worth. As I fucked her doggy style, I took one finger and gently pushed it in her asshole.

"Oh shit nigga, what you doin'?"

"You like that shit huh?"

"Hell yeah!"

I began to slowly fuck her ass with my finger, while I madly fucked her pussy.

"I like that shit baby do it again," she begged.

This time I slid my large finger in up to the third knuckle. She tensed up and screamed with lust as I rammed his finger up her ass and my dick in her pussy. I looked over and saw myself in her dresser mirror. I thought to myself, damn nigga, you look good as hell beatin this pussy up. I laid her flat on her stomach and slapped her ass with my dick a few times before back into sliding it into her again. I laid her almost flat on her back, as I fucked her. I gently pulled her hair, making her head extend backwards a bit so I could kiss her on the neck while I had my way with her. That sent her over the edge.

"I'm cummin, I'm cummin, don't stop! Hell yeah!" she cried as my dick plowed into her again and again. Her excitement got me right at the edge of exploding himself. I had to ask the patented Gerald question.

"Where you want it?" Without saying another word, she knew exactly what I was talking about.

"In my face boo, all over my muthafuckin face!"

I took a few more strokes. "Turn over, here it cum."

She turned over and opened her mouth, waiting for my load.

"Gimme that cum boo. I want it. I want to taste it boo, give it to me!" she said, as I stroked my erection.

"Ahh, damn baby, here you go. Get all of it. Let it run out your mouth."

She licked wildly at my dick trying not to miss a drop. She even gave it a few extra sucks to make sure she got all of it.

"Damn that was good," I said, while looking for my pants.

Nicole still lying on the bed asked "You leavin?"

"Yeah, I gotta lot to do in the morning."

"So that's it?" Her voice sounding more and more irritated with every word.

"You said you wanted to fuck and we did. What more do you want?"

Nicole had a strange look on her face as if she was not pleased at all. She sat there for another second or two looking confused.

"Aiight then, I guess I got what I wanted. Call me tomorrow," she said, as I walked towards the door.

"Yeah, I'll do that."

"Don't play with me," She said under her breath.

"What did you say?" I turned as trying to pretend I didn't hear what she said.

"Nothing, have a good one"

"Uh huh."

On the way home I thought about what she said. Don't play with me replayed over and over in my head.

"I be damned if I call your crazy ass again."

I don't mind sharing with anybody. But everybody has their thing they are just not gonna share. Mine happen to be my car. If you need a ride, I'll take you. If you need me to pick you up, I'll be there. But, to ask to borrow my car; just ain't gonna happen and Jay quickly found that out.

"Gerald, since you off tonight let me use the car to go to Destiny's house for a minute"

At first I started to act like I didn't hear him, hoping that he would catch the hint and not ask me again. But then he asked again, forcing me to answer him. I tried to be as delicate as I could.

"Hell no nigga! Nobody drives my car but me. I have the seat where I want it, the steering wheel at the right height, and the last thing I need is for one of my hoes to see my car over another bitch's house."

At first, I thought Jay was going to ask again but he just shook his head and looked at me like he was ready to beat my ass. We stood toe to toe staring at one another. The tension between us was thick and I was prepared to jump on his ass if he made any sudden moves. I owed him an ass whipping anyway.

"Fuck it man! I'll just have her come get me."

"Yeah you do that."

Jay walked out of the apartment and went and stood in the entranceway of our building. I guess he was trying to cool off. If he's that mad and need to cool off, he better get butt naked and stand in the middle of Antarctica before he tries some silly shit with me. I went and sat on the sofa and started watching my favorite show, Hell's Kitchen. Since I work on Tuesday nights I have to DVR it and watch it on my off days. As I sat there, I couldn't help but think about Jay. I know he wanted to beat my ass. In a one on one fight, he probably could beat my ass, but I'll never let him know I think that. I've heard him on the phone tell someone that he hates the way I talk to him, but he feels trapped because he's living in my house. If I put him out, he wouldn't have any place to lay his head so he just takes my verbal abuse. But, I'm not stupid. I know to sleep with one eye open.

As Jay stood outside waiting on Destiny to come pick him up, I decided to take another opportunity to get into Jay's head.

"Look man, I know you think I don't like your girl. To be honest with you, you're right, but I do have one good thing to say about her."

Jay just looked up at me with a what the hell grin across his face.

"What's that?"

"I have noticed that Destiny has as the roundest ass I've ever seen," holding up my fist for a fist bump with my boy.

Jay started smiling then answered, "Yeah dawg that ass is huge, but I tell you what. The pussy looks even better."

I knew that Jay was the type of guy that always told the fellas how good his girl was in bed, and all the freaky things they like to do. So it was always easy for all the boys to take his women throughout the years. But for some reason, Jay couldn't catch on to what we were doing to him. He would even go so far as to tell the fellas all the women likes and dislikes.

"She rides dick like she's in the rodeo. She sucks my balls, plays with my ass, everything! Anything I want her to do she does. I say I want to cum in her face, I do it. I say I want to fuck her in the ass, I do it. She's a freak! I know I said I was starting to catch feeling for her, but dawg, she is off the hook. Not the kind of chick you take home to mama."

I knew he would open up, but he just told me all of her business. Hell, it even sparked a small interest in my mind. My brain is like a mini recorder. Everything Jay said, I stored it away. All the while laughing with Jay, as he told me about Destiny.

"Then, after we fuck she wants to lay up in bed and tell me all the things she look for in a man. All the qualities she requires. "

"Like what?" I asked, desperately wanting to know more.

"She wants a man that will make her laugh when she's down, A man that will pamper her every now and then. I damn near lost it when she said she wants the type of man that will surprise her with small gifts, nothing expensive, but little sweet things. When she is getting out the shower, she wants her man to have a nice thick drying towel in the dryer, get it nice and warm, and wrap it around her as she steps out of the shower. Ain't that some shit?"

In my mind that actually sounded kinda nice. I have to remember that one, I thought to myself, as Jay continued to talk.

"Don't get me wrong, I'm feeling her, but some of the shit that she wants me to do is a little much for a nigga like me."

"So let me ask you a question, Mr. Lover Man. Are you serious about a girl that will lick your ass, after you meet her on the party line?" I asked, hoping for the answer I was looking for.

One thing you have to understand, is when you and the fellas are playing several women, you have to have rules. One rule is if you say that you and a certain woman are kicking it seriously, all hands are off her. Even if you are running around on her, if you claim that one girl, everybody else has to back off. If you are asked if you and your girl are serious and you say no, then any person in the group can go after her. Even wild animals have rules they follow.

Since Jay knew that I didn't like Destiny at all. He played it like he was starting to lose feeling for her a little.

"Nah man. She's cool an all, but we aint serious or nothing like that. The pussy good but lately the dog in me has begun to bark again."

That was just what I wanted to hear.

"Since the dog in you is coming back, tell her ass to stop coming around here so fucking much. A nigga can't even walk around the house scratching my balls without making sure she's not sitting in the front room."

We both laughed a little. I was about to say her ass had to start paying rent since she was over the house so much.

Jay just shook his head, "I feel you. Yeah man, I'll handle that."

At that moment, Destiny drove up in the parking lot. She was about to get out the car when Jay waved his hand at her telling her to stay there.

"Handle your business playa," I coached, as Jay walked towards the waiting car.

Once in the car, Jay leaned over and kissed Destiny on her ruby red full lips.

"Hey baby, where you want to go?" Destiny asked, sounding enthusiastic from just being near Jay.

"I don't care as long as it keeps us out the house for a minute."

"What happened? What did dick head say this time?"

"He said you're over the house too much."

Destiny was visibly upset. "You know what Jay ? Fuck him and you!"

Jay sat straight up in the seat looking stunned by her words.

"Why it gotta be all that? I didn't say it, he did."

"Well you might as well have been the one to say it; since you didn't stand up for me in front of him!"

"Well, what do you want me to say?"

"Tell him that you pay rent there just like he does and he should respect you just the same as you respect him." Destiny was not one for holding back once she was angry.

"You acting like a little bitch!"

Jay's eyes widened as she continued.

"That's right nigga, I said it! You're acting like a little scared bitch. Whatever that nigga say, you do it. I bet if he told you to break up with me, you'd do it."

Jay was furious by the way she was talking to him.

"Don't you ever talk to me like that again. You hear me! Who the fuck do you think you are?"

Destiny turned down the radio to make sure that Jay heard what she had to say.

"Oh you'll jump bad at me, but you'll bitch up when it comes to you boy, right?"

"It ain't that serious, so stop trippin alright."

Jay would not go up against Gerald even in college. Gerald has intimidated Jay for some reason. Gerald had a certain swagger about himself that demanded respect from everybody in a room. He was loud and very outspoken. Those qualities often made people back down when confronted by him.

"It is that serious! I can't go to MY man's house to see MY man because MY man's bitch ass daddy said I was coming by too much.

Destiny is getting madder and madder by the second.

"That's bullshit, fuck that nigga. I'll go over there when the fuck I want to. And that nigga know betta to say that bullshit to, ole punk!"

"He's my boy, he took me in when I couldn't go back to Miami after I graduated. My mother and I didn't get along to well and I had no place else to go so that punk as you called him got my back".

Jay felt like he owed a lot to Gerald for being by his side when everybody else in his life walked away from him.

"That's my dawg and regardless of what you say, he will always be my dawg."

Destiny was not trying to hear all that.

"Do you pay rent there?"

"Yes."

"Then it's your damn house too. I don't give a damn whos name is on the lease, you pay, I stay. Fuck him!"

"Calm down, I'll talk to him 'bout it tomorrow. Besides, I have a bone to pick with him anyway about something he said earlier. Let's just do what we do tonight."

With that, Jay walked over to a still shaking mad Destiny and gently kissed her on the neck. He could feel her start to calm down as he rubbed over her very large breasts. Her nipples had started to poke thru her bra and you could see them thru her shirt. She reached back and felt his dick start to stiffen in her hands. He lifted her shirt over her head and unhooked her bra. From behind, he grabbed both her breasts and squeezed them in his hands. He dropped to his knees behind her and ran his tongue up her spine very slowly. As he stood up, she arched her back so her ass would push right into his crotch. She turned around to face him unzipping his pants.

"Let's 69," she asked hoping that he would finally taste her. It has been 6 months and he has yet to even attempt to perform oral sex on her.

"Baby, you know I don't do that"

Instant anger ran through her with that statement.

"But it's o.k. for me to suck your dick right?" She paused for a minute, "let's try this," she said in a very sarcastic voice."I don't do you till you do me. How 'bout that?"

"So now we are gonna be childish. I'll do you, if you do me," he said sounding like a 9 year old school boy.

"You call it what you want. But your dick will be dry till you do".

She put back on her shirt "Let's go, I'm taking you home to be with your boy!"

I don't know what it is about Destiny, but every time I see her, I just want to run up to her, bend her over and fuck the shit out of her. Don't get me wrong, I'm still as wild with the women as I've ever been. After I used up my first initial 90 minutes on the party line it's been costing me $40.00 for every 4 hours I was on the line. It had gotten to the point where I was budgeting in money for the line out of my paycheck. I felt addicted to it. That $40.00 would last me an entire week.

Tonight is a new night, which means a new woman for me. My goal is to sleep with at least three women during a seven-day period. So far, I am meeting my quota. My night started off just as the others had, me with a hard dick looking to put it into someone.

"What's your name again sweetheart?" I asked, sounding cocky as hell.

"Gina"

"What are you looking for on the line?"

"Well, a good friend."

"No, seriously, what are you looking for, because I'm looking for a female that want to get into something tonight."

It had gotten to the point where I felt like all I had to do was say my name, and women were suppose to drop their clothes and hop in bed with me. It's not my fault they are giving up the ass so easy. I feel like there is no need in trying to get to know a woman when I didn't really want to get to know them anyway.

"Damn, since it's like that, yeah I might be looking to get into something tonight myself."

"So what time will you be over?"

"Hold up. You don't know me from Adam but you want me to come over to your place?"

The one thing I cannot stand is a mouthy woman. She and I both know she want to fuck tonight. So why does she want to play this game?

"You just said you were looking to get into something tonight, right?

"Yeah, but…"

"So, I'm down to make something happen if you are. I'm tall, dark and all man, all day. Come over here and I'm certain you've leave with the world's biggest smile on your face."

"Damn, you're confident," she paused for a second "alright, I'll come by there"

"How soon can you be here? I need you to be here ASAP since I now have something to prove."

Gina laughed, and then answered "I can be there in 30 minutes if that's cool with you?"

"Yea, that's cool but do you have anything sexy to wear? I'm a visual type of guy, and seeing a beautiful woman in something sexy is a huge turn on for me."

"I have a few things I could put on to make sure you give me what I'm coming over there for."

This conversation was going just how I wanted it to. I knew that I had another female to lie up with for the night.

"Describe what you are going to wear for me."

I sat on the edge of my bed and listened as Gina told me the sexy outfit she was planning to put on.

"I have this red and black corset with a matching red thong, I like to wear on special occasions. It has the garters and all with it. I like to wear a nice pair of black stockings and black heels when I wear that outfit."

My dick instantly jumped up when I heard her talk about her corset.

"That sounds good as hell. I look forward to seeing you in that"

Gina was an early Christmas present to myself. It was cold outside and nothing is better than cuddling up to a nice thick body under a nice comforter. The apartment I live in has a fire place that was perfect for making the ladies think this was a romantic evening when it was nothing more than a set up for a quick fuck.

"I never got this much pussy before in my life," I said to myself, while walking into the bathroom to take a shower. As I turned the water on in the shower, Nicole ran across my mind. Talking to myself, "I bet that bitch mad as hell right about now. Got fucked and dumped all in the same night, by the same nigga."

************************************

The erratic driving must have shook me enough to wake me. I felt myself trying to open my eyes. I must have passed out because the next thing I knew I'm in the back of an ambulance. All I can hear now is muffled sounds. My girl is still by my side. I love her more than anything on the planet. Then it hit me, I wonder if that crazy bitch had something to do with this. Then I felt myself going out again.

************************************

"I got something for his ass." Nicole was fuming "come over here, fuck me and never holla at me again. Oh hell nah. That nigga must have bumped his fucking head if he thinks I'm a let that shit ride." As tears of anger rolled down her face, all she could think about was hurting Gerald in some way. She knew that she was too small to fight him, but she had other ways of getting back at him.

"I told him not to play with me, all he had to do was call me and his sorry ass couldn't do that. He wouldn't even return my calls".

She grabbed her car keys and headed out the door.

\*\*\*\*\*\*\*\*\*\*\*\*\*\*\*\*\*\*\*\*\*\*\*\*\*\*\*\*\*\*\*\*\*\*\*\*\*\*\*\*

After my shower, I was getting ready for Gina to arrive. I stood in the mirror as I've has done several time admiring himself.

"Damn nigga, you aiight, if I was a female I'd fuck you," I said to myself with laughter.

While standing there in a wrap around cloth on my lower half and a tank top shirt, the phone started to ring. Looking at the caller I.D, "that crazy bitch Nicole again. When will she catch the hint that I don't want anything to do with her silly ass?"

As I walked away from the phone, there was a knock at the door

"Damn it's been thirty minutes already?"

Figuring I would not need clothes anyway, I answered the door in the wrap and T-shirt.

"How are you tonight?" I asked the beautiful, sexy ass woman at the door.

"Better now that I know what's on your mind. Do you always answer the door half naked?"

"Only when I'm expecting a fine ass woman to be half naked with me."

The two of us moved towards the sofa. She undid my wrap and it fell to the floor unveiling my already half-hard dick.

"You wearing what you told me you would?" I asked, standing in front of Gina with a now fully erect dick.

With that, she unzipped her jean skirt and let it fall to the floor. I was amazed at how thick her thighs were. The sight of her thick body was intoxicating. She slowly took off her sweater. And there she stood all 5'6 inches of a chocolate thick Goddess in a red and black corset and thong set with heels to help set it off.

Her breasts were full with nipples the size of nickels. As I sat on the sofa and began to stroke myself slowly, she turned around and showed me her large, apple shaped ass. Her long black hair swung all over her back, as she danced like a stripper in the club and rotated her hips for my enjoyment.

"You are fine as hell boo," is all I could say as she performed for me. I had never seen a woman so beautiful, so perfect. "Let me ask you a question?"

She turned around still dancing now facing me sucking on her own breast and rubbing her body.

"Why are you on the chat line? I know you have no problems finding a man, as fine as you are."

She walked over to me and pressed her breast into my face while answering me.

"On the line I can fuck as much as I want, I don't have to answer to anybody, and the dick is always available when and if I want it."

With that, she took of my shirt and began licking my chest as I grabbed her breast. She pushed my hands off of her. "Don't touch, just enjoy."

I laid back in the chair and took in all she had to offer. She flung one leg over my lap and slowly lowered herself onto my now throbbing dick. We fucked like wild animals; in different positions, on the sofa, the kitchen chairs, and the floor in front of the fireplace. She laid on my chest propped herself up with straight arms and rode my dick making her ass cheeks clap every time she came up never taking off her heels or corset.

"I'm 'bout to cum baby!" I yelled, as she jumped off my dick. She removed the condom and sucked me as I came in her mouth. It never seems to amaze me at what these women will do after talking to a guy for about 5 minutes on the telephone. She went into the bathroom to spit out my offerings. Giggling to myself, "The date line strikes again. " She returned from the bathroom and started picking up her things.

"I gotta go," she said nonchalantly.

"Aiight then," as I handed her, her thong. She stuffed them into her purse and pulled her jean skirt up.

"Zip me up please," turning around so I could zip her skirt up from the back.

"My girls and I are going to the club, come up there if you get a chance."

"I'll see what I can do. I'll walk you out."

I could not have been more pleased with myself. I had fucked another woman, and this time she left without me feeling like I had done her wrong.

We walked outside in the frigate air when I noticed..

"What the fuck happened to my car!" I screamed, as I ran over to my car. The back window was shattered and a brick was lying on the back seat. I looked around to see if anyone was outside and saw nothing.

"I know who did this. I'm a kill that bitch".

Gina was unfazed by the sight of the car.

"I guess one of your bitches trying to tell you something," she said, as she got in her car.

"I'm gonna tell her ass something, with my foot when I catch up to her."

I stood there with tears in my eyes I was so angry. I kicked the tires and damned Nicole's name. Gina drove off and went on her way when my cell phone rang,

"I saw you and your little bitch outside tonight," I turned around hoping to see Nicole.

"Where you at bitch? I'm gonna fuck you up for breaking my window."

"I didn't break shit! If I did it I would have stayed there and waited for your punk ass to come outside and see it."

I walked around the car mad as hell. I was hot enough to spit fire.

"And you wonder why I never called your silly ass back, because you stupid. I could tell you weren't shit when I fucked you. Fuckin Skank!"

Laughing in a very irritating way she answered back, "That's all right you are getting what your ass deserve. I hope when you get in your car that bitch blow up."The phone suddenly went silent.

"Ahhhhhh, I hate that bitch!" I screamed, as I stared at my now messed up car. In my mind, I wondered if I got in the car and started the engine, if it really would blow up.

"Damn I hate that bitch!"

With a loud pop, my ears finally felt like the bubble that was in them had burst. I could finally hear again. The very first voice I heard belonged to my girl.

"Baby you're going to be ok. They are going to take good care of you. When you get out I'll be right here waiting for you."

I looked over at her as she walked quickly next to the gurney I was being pushed on. The ceiling was white and it had to be about three nurses and two doctors all wearing scrubs and blue scrub caps; talking and walking in stride with the fast moving gurney. A slight smile cracked my face. I have no clue what's going on but for some reason all I can think about is the story Jay told me about a Christmas present.

***********************************

"Jay, since you are going home for Christmas tomorrow, I'll come and pick you up so I can give you your Christmas present tonight at my house, alright?" Destiny said, sounding extremely happy.

Since their last big fight about Gerald, Jay had straightened out a bit and told Gerald that Destiny was able to call whenever she pleased because he paid rent there also. That conversation didn't go over well with Gerald at all, but he let it ride cause he knew in his head that her calling the house would not be an issue too much longer.

"What time will you be here? Gerald and I have a little bit of running around to do tonight."

With pure joy in her voice, "I'll be there around 8."

"Make it 9."

"OK, I'll talk to you later."

"Bye."

Jay needed that extra hour to freshen up after Tonya left. Tonya was a very thin, very light skinned, no shape girl that

Jay had met on the line a few weeks back. She was a college sophomore at the local college. Her young slender body was new to sex and since she's been on the line, became addicted to it. She fucked for the attention. Tonya was the type of girl that did whatever with who ever. It didn't matter where the sex was at, she had to have it. The news got out about her doing anybody on her campus and she's been very popular with the guys ever since. She likes to use the phrase," I have more male friends than I do female friends because females start and keep shit going". That was just her way to say that she's fucking any guy that walks up and hold a conversation with her for more than three minutes.

Whenever Jay had a girl over, if Gerald had nothing to do, he would just stay in his room and let Jay handle his business in the front room on the floor. Gerald had a rule. Nobody fucks on the sofa but him, and since they lived in a one-bedroom apartment that meant the floor was wide open for Jay to use all he wanted.

"You gotta go," Gerald heard Jay tell Tonya,"Me and my boy are playing spades in here with some friends tonight and they'll be here in a few, so I'll holla at you later." Tonya knew her role to leave without a fuss. She grabbed up her things and sat on the sofa to get dressed. Just then Gerald walked into the front room.

"If you don't get your narrow naked ass off my sofa!" he screamed, as Tonya damn near jumped out of her skin. She had already told Jay that Gerald intimidated her, so she jumped off the sofa and got dressed right in front of both of them. Just to make sure that Tonya really felt bad, Gerald started up a conversation about other women right in front of her standing there getting dressed. The look of Tonya's face was pure humiliation. She walked over to Jay "I'm 'bout to go," she said, as she reached out her hand to rub his bare chest.

Jay quickly pushed her hand down and in a very irritated voice and answered her, "Aiight then, bye," motioning his head towards the door, as if telling her to hit the street.

Gerald stood to the door and opened it as Tonya approached. Tonya looked up at Gerald, like he was the school's principal.

"See you later Gerald," Tonya said, out of nervousness.

"Beat it," Gerald replied, as he slammed the door behind her. Without even thinking twice about how much he had just humiliated Tonya, Gerald struck up a conversation with Jay.

"Playing it close ain't you?" Gerald asked, as he walked away from the door. "You gave yourself fifteen minutes before Destiny pick you up."

"That's the way playas play," Jay sang, like he was a part of Junior Mafia.

Gerald sat on the sofa and noticed a red box lying on the floor.

"What's in the box?"

"Destiny's Christmas gift."

"What is it?" Gerald asked, wanting to know what Jay's broke ass could afford.

"It's a book."

"You got your girl a book for Christmas? I sure as hell hope it's one she wanted to read," Gerald said, laughing a little. He thought to himself, she is gonna eat his ass up if he gives her a fucking book for Christmas.

"She'll love it, trust me."

"Did she ask for it?"

"No, why?"

Gerald turned away and started walking towards his room, "Nothing man. I'm sure she'll really get a kick out of it," then he mumbled under his breath,"Or she's gonna kick your ass; one or the other."

A few minutes later, there was a knock at the door. Jay opened it and saw that it was Destiny.

"Hey baby, how you doing?" She asked, as she started walking into the apartment.

"I'm good." Jay walked over and picked the box up of the floor. Destiny's eyes lit up as she stared at the box.

"What's in the box?" Destiny asked, sounding excited.

"You'll find out later."

Twenty minutes later, they arrived at Destiny's house. She opened the door and Jay walked in ahead of her. His eyes almost jumped out of his head when he saw the large gift-wrapped box sitting on the sofa.

"Would you like to exchange gifts now or after dinner?" she asked.

From the size of the box, Jay knew that she had gotten him something that was a lot more expensive than his book. He started to feel a little ashamed of his gift. Gerald's voice played again and again in his head, "I damn sure hope she asked for a book".

"Well, what do you want to do?" Destiny asked again, as Jay just stood there with a blank look on his face.

"We can wait till later. As a matter of fact, let's not open gifts till Christmas. I've never liked opening gifts before they are supposed to be opened."

"No, I want to open gifts tonight. Besides, I can't wait till you see what I got you. You're gonna love it! "

"You are enough for me baby. I don't need anything else." Jay said, trying to ease the blow he knew he had coming.

"You're so sweet." Destiny was all smiles after hearing that.

An hour after Jay and Destiny had dinner they decided to exchange gifts.

Jay tried everything from faking like he had gotten sick to pretending that he picked up the wrong gift to try and get out of exchanging gifts with Destiny. She walked over to the couch and put his present right in his lap. He just sat there speechless.

"Well go ahead and open the box silly!" She said, as she sat in the chair across from him to make sure she would be able to see the look on his face when he opened the box.

Jay lifted the top off the box and automatically knew what it was. The smell of it gave it away even before he could pull the white inside wrap paper back to reveal what the gift was. Jay's mouth fell open as he pulled the Sean John Collection leather jacket from the box.

"Oh my God baby! How much did you spend on this jacket?" Jay asked, putting the jacket on and running to the mirror to see how he looked in it.

"Don't worry 'bout how much I paid for it. I saw it and wanted you to have it."

Destiny sat and waited until Jay had finished running around looking at himself in every mirror in the house. He sat back down at the table and then reality set in and set in fast. It was time for him to give Destiny her gift.

"I hope you like it," he said, as he reluctantly handed her the box.

Destiny tore into the box like a child on Christmas morning. Her eyes were big as marbles as she tossed the inside white wrap paper to the side.

"A family history tree record book!" she said with disbelief and shock in her voice. She looked at Jay and wanted to ask him what the hell was he thinking, but she was a real good woman about it.

"Thanks baby, I'll put it to good use." In her head she was thinking yeah as soon as it starts to snow this fucking book is going into the fireplace.

A giant smile ran across Jay's face. "I knew you'd like it. You always talkin' about you wish you could track your roots, now you can." Jay was happy that he didn't get his ass beat like Gerald had predicted.

Destiny sat there and looked at the book wanting to throw it at him, but she kept her composure.

Thinking to herself, does this nigga really think he did some-thing? I gave his ass a Sean John Collection leather jacket and he gave me a fucking book. Not just any old book, a fuckin book that I have to write in."

To keep from exploding all over his ass, she changed the topic.

"So when does your plane land back here?" she asked him, trying hard to remain calm after that gift.

"I land at 6:00 p.m. next Thursday. I'm flying Delta but my plane has a layover in Atlanta. So look for flight number 5509 arriving from Atlanta."

"OK, I'll be there to pick you up. When does your boy get back in town?" she asked, just to be nosey.

"He's comin back next Friday night."

"Let me have your key when I drop you off in the morning for your flight. I want to have something special planned for you when you get back."

Jay, not passing up the opportunity to have Destiny all to himself in the house gave her the key. Without realizing he was talking out loud

"Hell if you want, we can even fuck in his bed, have his ass layin in my nutt," Jay joked. Destiny didn't laugh at Jay's joke partly because she was still a little pissed off about the gift and secondly she thought that was just nasty.

Jay on the other hand was starting to get a little tired of Gerald's demanding ways. Destiny was constantly in his ear about standing up to Gerald. He had already started doing little things around the apartment to get under Gerald's skin. This would be a good way to really get at him. Jay was so caught up in his own world of Gerald lying in his nut, that he didn't realize that Destiny was looking at him with utter disgust on her face.

A last minute change of plans forced me not to go home for the holidays. For the most part, I just sat in the apartment enjoying the fact that I was there alone. No Jay getting on my damn nerves. I didn't even get on the party line for the entire week. I just wanted to sit at home and relax. I walked into the kitchen to grab me a Strawberry Pop Tart and a glass of milk. Now that I think about it, this is the first time since Jay moved in that I was able to get a pop tart after Wednesday. Normally his greedy ass would have eaten them all by now. As I poured the milk I heard keys at the door. I knew Jay was not due back until tomorrow. So I slowly walked over to the door and grabbed a steel rod that I kept next to the door, just in case a nigga decided to try to come up in my shit. I stood close against the wall and waited for the intruder to come into the apartment. I had always heard that if you kill a nigga for trying to come up in your house that they had to be inside the house in order to not catch that charge, but if they were outside, then you were going down for murder. How true that Is, I don't know, but I knew I wasn't gonna take a chance. I was going to wait until this muthafucka got all the way into the apartment and bash his fucking brains out. The door opened, my heart started beating faster and faster. I knew the time was approaching for me to handle my business. I'm not gonna lie, I was scared but fear was my friend at this moment. Fear is what's gonna make me do what I have to do. I saw the foot of the intruder cross the threshold. I gripped the rod tighter in my hand. I wanted to make sure I had the perfect grip on it. I didn't want it to go flying out of my hand while I was trying to hit this muthafucka. I raised the rod over my head. Then I heard the strangest thing. A female voice was speaking.

"I can't wait for Jay to come back in town. It's gonna be off the hook. Light the fire, cook a little dinner, and have crazy sex."

She reached for the light switch and I grabbed her arm and started my downward swing with the rod. Her eyes were as big as baseballs and it took everything in me to stop the flow of the swing I had produced. She dropped her keys and tried to cover her face with her free hand.

Still holding on to her arm I started screaming.

"What the hell are you doing over here?" Before she could answer I started again. "Who gave you a fucking key to my house? Answer me!"

I couldn't let on that she scared the shit out of me and from the look on her face I knew I had damn near scared the piss out of her. We both stood there and stared at one another for a second or two.

She finally spoke up, "What are you doing here? I thought you went out of town."

"That's what you get for thinking! I didn't go home I had to work. How da hell did you get a key?" He asked, wondering what was going on. Destiny, still a little shaken didn't know what to say.

"I was gonna straighten up a little to surprise Jay when he got home. Since y'all niggas only clean up every 3 months or when the pile of chicken wing bones next to the sofa accidentally gets kicked over." The more she talked the more her dislike for me became more evident. "Now that's it's just you and I here, I can tell you what's been on my mind." I guess she saw this as a grand opportunity to finally tell me what she thought of me. Her eyes started to widen and her fist clinched like she was ready to knock my head clean off my shoulders. "Who the fuck are you to tell me I can't come over here, when man pays half the rent and only sleeps on the couch! My man pays half the phone and I can't call? He asked you to bring him to my house and you said no, after he put gas in your raggedy ass car."

I started to lock horns with this mad ass woman right there on the spot but something about her was turning me on real fast. I don't know if it was the fact that she was mad as hell, something about a pissed off sista is always sexy to me, or the fact that she was standing up to me which is something that most people don't do. I decided now was my time to go for the jugular. I was owed and I was about to collect on an old debt. Jay owed me and he was about to pay me without knowing it.

Screaming from the top of my lungs it just came out.

"I did all that to protect you!"

Destiny face instantly turned into the what the fuck are you talking about look. I knew I had her full attention at this point. I must admit that round ass of hers was always a turn on. Not to mention she was beautiful. I mean drop dead beautiful. She was way out of Jay's league. So I figured, I'd do him a favor and keep him from looking stupid later.

"See, I didn't want you to come over here and get your heart broke."

Destiny looked at him with a confused look on her face. "What are you talking 'bout, you did what to protect me?"

"I said for you to stop calling, thinking that you would eventually lose interest in Jay."   Anger filled the room again, after she heard those words.

"That's fucked up Gerald, and you know it! Why are you trying to hurt your boy?"

I slowly walked over to Destiny and stood right in her face.

"I'm not trying to hurt him. Like I said I'm trying to protect you. Your boy has been fuckin everyday since y'all met. I know you think that I'm the dog, but it's not me."

Destiny stood motionless. I could tell she didn't know whether to believe me or not, but the truth had to be told or at least my version of it.

"He and I have had foursomes with different women several times in the last few weeks. He's even fuckin this white girl that work at IHOP."

Tears began rolling down Destiny's face as she listened to the words falling from my lips "You making this shit up,

Gerald! You a low ass nigga for trying to break us up! You ain't shit!"

She tried to walk away from me, but I was right behind her reaching for her hand.

"I didn't know you two were a couple. I asked him the other day if he was serious about you and he said no."

Right then the mean hard look in Destiny's face went soft. I could tell I was starting to get to her.

"He said he was with you because you would do whatever he asked you to do in the bedroom."

Destiny's mouth fell open, "What did he tell you about me?"

"I know all about you playing with his ass, suckin his dick and when did black girls get into ass fucking?"

Tears were now flowing down Destiny's face. Embarrassment and humiliation was all over the place. She caught herself gagging a few times trying not to throw up. She stumbled as she looked for a chair to sit down.

There was no sense in holding back now. I might as well let it all out in the open. "How do you think I know all this about you? I know your favorite color, food, and book. Sexual position, everything."

I walked over to her and put my hand on her back as she laid her head on the table.

"You are way too special to be with a nigga like that."

Destiny looked up at him with complete defeat in her eyes. She had given her all to Jay and he had betrayed her.

"Why would he do this to me?" She asked, wanting answers.

"That's the kinda nigga he's always been. Since we were in college he's done this to countless women." My hands found their way to her back and was now rubbing her in a comforting brotherly way. Destiny was crying uncontrollably,

"Wait till his ass get back! I'm gonna…"

I cut her off, "You're gonna remain a lady; a beautiful respectable lady. Don't let a nigga like that bring you down. Don't let him make you act less that a woman. He wants you to be down in the gutter with him. Don't give him the satisfaction."

I knew just what to say to make her feel good about herself. "You're a beautiful woman, a class act. Any man would love to have you for himself. You're more than just some nigga's boo or wifey. You the kinda female that a man will come home right after work to get with. The kinda woman that when you are getting out the shower, he's there with a warm towel right out the dryer to wrap around your cold body."

While her head was on the table, I began to smile devilishly, telling her what Jay told me she said. She was too upset to recognize her own words being used against her.

Suddenly Destiny jumped up from the table.

"I gotta go," she said, as she got up to leave. I couldn't let her leave. I knew if she did she was going to try to find a way to talk to Jay and I couldn't have that. But I guess Mother Nature was on my side because snow started falling.

"It's starting to snow pretty hard outside. You can stay here for the night if you want. I'll sleep out here and you can sleep in my room. Give me a minute to change the sheets."

Destiny looked out the window and it was coming down hard outside. Hesitantly, she replied, "No, I'll sleep out here I don't want to kick you out your own bed."

"It's not a problem at all. It's the least I can do, after all that you've been through tonight."

I saw a slight smile start on one side of her face. I knew I had her at that point.

Destiny and I sat in the front room and talked for hours. For the first time since we've been knowing each other, we finally were able to sit down and talk like humans.

Her cell phone rang several times with a 305 area code. She knew it was Jay, but she refused to take the call. We talked about our younger school days, first dates and our families.

With a smile on her face, she said, "I didn't know you where this cool," as I sat across from her, trying to pick the right moment to make my move.

"You never took the time to know me. You just took Jay at his word and automatically started hating me."

Destiny smiled wider. "I don't hate you. I dislike some of your ways."

"I'm just a man that knows what I want out of life and I work hard to get it. If I see something I want, I go after it. My personality sometimes intimidates people, but those are the people that don't understand me. They cannot handle a person like me. I need a woman that can hold her own in a conversation, a woman that has a backbone, a woman that is not afraid to say what's on her mind. I made a promise to God that if he provided me with the right woman I would stop doing all the things that I do. I'm just looking for the perfect woman for me. I know she's out there."

I knew I had just described Destiny to the letter and she knew it as well. Her mind was racing a mile a minute trying to process everything that was going on around her. She was just told that the man she was dealing with was cheating and lying to her, and the man she hated was everything she ever wanted.

"This is way too much for me tonight. I'm gonna go ahead and call it a night." She said, as she stood up and walked into the kitchen to grab something to drink. I saw this as my golden opportunity.

"I have some sweat pants and sweat shirt in the room that I've never worn if you want to take a shower instead of sleeping in those clothes."

I could tell she was kinda scared, but I did everything I could to make her feel at ease. "Look, I'm not going to rape you or anything like that. I just want you to be comfortable."

She took me up on my offer.

"Here's a wash cloth," I said, as I handed her the sweats and the towel. As soon as I heard the shower start, I took a very fluffy towel and put it in the dryer. About twenty minutes into her shower

"Gerald!" Destiny hollered from the inside of the bathroom. "You forgot to give me a drying towel." I went to the dryer took the towel out.

"Hear you go" I cracked the door and handed her the warm towel. She looked at me with disbelief, gave me the biggest smile and closed the door.

After she got out the shower, I was still playing the best man roll.

"Well, I see that you are comfortable. I'm gonna head to bed now. You sure you don't want to sleep in my bed and I'll sleep out here. It's not a problem."

"No, I appreciate the offer but I think I'll be alright."

"Ok then, good night." I walked down the hallway to my bedroom. I stopped at the air conditioner thermostat and turned the heat off. With it snowing outside, it's going to get really cold, real fast. I went into my room and closed the door. Normally I lock the door but tonight I left the door unlocked just in case. About three hours after I had went to sleep.

"Gerald wake up, do you have another comforter it's getting kinda cold out there."

I looked up and saw Destiny standing over me completely naked. My eyes could have popped out of my head at the sight of her. I flung the cover back. I turned the heat off to get her to come into my room, but damn, this shit worked out better that what I thought.

"Yeah, come lay down with me, it's nice and warm under here."

She laid down next to me and we began to kiss and rub all over one another. Destiny was still hurt by the story she was told about Jay. She wanted to hurt him in a way only fucking his boy could hurt. I knew that Jay did not perform oral sex on her, so that was the first thing I did. I tucked my head under the sheet and spread her legs apart. The thought of being eaten out again after so long, was enough to almost make her cum with the slightest touch. I licked her inner thighs and slowly moved up to her freshly shaved pussy. I licked her fat labia lips gently. I took my thumb and index finger and opened her up. Her pussy was as pink as a carnation. I took my tongue and licked around her lips before finding her clit.

"Right there baby," she whispered, as I took my time eating her. I flicked my tongue over her clit as fast as I could, making her arch her back and beg for more. I nibbled and sucked on her clit for what seemed like twenty minutes. Destiny moaned and came over and over again on my face. I even took it one-step further; I put her in the doggy style position and continued to eat her from the back. This time, it was not her pussy I was eating, it was her ass. She had never had that done before.

"Damn baby, that feels good." I fucked her ass with my tongue, making her cum again. After countless orgasms, Destiny turned around and asked me to stand up. I stood with my dick aimed right at her mouth. She opened her mouth and let me slid my thick dick right into her face. I was much bigger than Jay and she was excited about it. She licked the head of my dick quickly with her tongue. She circled the head with her tongue while spitting all over my dick. Every time she took my dick out of her mouth, she let a long thick string of spit fall from my dick to her chest. She sucked my balls gently while stroking my dick.

"So, this is what I've been missing," she said, right before stuffing as much of my dick into her mouth as she could. I got on top of Destiny and was ready to go in for the kill.

"Hold up Gerald."

"Why? What's wrong?"

"It's just that when we get together I want it to be because we want it to happen. Not because I'm pissed off at Jay."

Damn now I had to think fast on my feet. I'm at the door and its open, all I have to do is go in and enjoy the ride.

"I fully understand that. As a matter of fact, that just made me respect you even more."

"I hope you're not mad at me?" She said, rubbing my chest.

"No baby, I'm not mad at all. If you want to wait, I'll wait. But I do have a request."

Destiny looked at him a little awkward.

"Yeah what is it?"

"Can I at least hold you till you fall asleep?"

Destiny's face lit up. She backed into him and allowed him to hold her as she fell asleep.

The next morning, I slipped out of bed and went to the McDonalds up the street to surprise Destiny. I even knew what she likes to eat from there. She was surprised when she was awakened by the smell of Hash Browns and a Sausage, Egg and Cheese McGriddle. We sat in bed and ate breakfast. Destiny could not help but think about Jay. A large smile went across her face.

"What's on your mind babe? Something got you smiling,"

She looked over at me and rubbed my face. "It's nothing, I just thought about something I have to do."

Sitting in the waiting room in this hospital is driving me crazy. When this day started, I had no clue or would have even imagined that it would end like this. My mind cannot help but wonder what could have caused all of this to happen. What would make a person act out in such a way?

**************************************

Flight number 5509 arriving from Atlanta had just touched down when chills started running down my spine.

What am I gonna say when I see him? I thought to myself.

Just be cool play it off like nothing is wrong, I told myself repeatedly.

As Jay walked down the airport landing tunnel, it was obvious that he had no idea what transpired while he was out of town. His face lit up when he saw me standing there ready to greet him. He had no clue, Gerald had betrayed his trust. No idea that I knew everything that he had told Gerald about me and all the women he had been sleeping with.

"Hey baby how was your flight?" I asked as Jay walked up to me throwing his arms around me and holding me tight. I was a little surprised at the open public affection Jay was showing me. That was something that he hated. He would never show his soft side in public.

"It was aiight, Gerald told me before that for some reason, it's always a bumpy landing in Greensboro. So you ready for our special night?"

Just the mention of Gerald's name made me think about that tongue lashing he put on me last night..."Yeah I'm ready," I finally answered, but what I wanted to say was hell no I don't ever want you touching me again you childish bastard. In the car on the way back to his apartment, Jay opened up to me like never before.

"You know, while I was home I had a long talk with my mother about you."

"Really? What did y'all talk about?"

"Well, I told her that I was in love."

I almost drove the car over the overpass on the highway.

"You're in love? With who?"

"You, I'm ready to tell the world how I feel about you. I want everyone to know that you are mine and I'm yours."

Now ain't this about a bitch. Now he wants to step his game up. Part of me wants to believe him and go with what he's talking about, but I just cannot forget about all the shit he told Gerald about me. He put all my business in the street.

"You know your boy is at home right?" I boldly announced. I never took my eyes off the road to see his reaction to me not responding to his sudden show of affection.

"What the hell is he doing there? He's not supposed to be back till tomorrow."

"Surprised me too when I walked in trying to set things up for tonight."

I could tell Jay got nervous. Beads of sweat popped up on his forehead. He looked around like the law was chasing him and his throat cracked when he spoke.

"You talked to him?"

"Yeah, we talked."

Jay's hands started to fidget a little. He nervously looked out the window and then back at me. "About what?" he asked, looking like a crack head feigning for his next hit.

"Oh, nothing much really, just.....YOU."

All of a sudden it was like watching a cartoon character turn 100 different colors after eating something or smelling some-thing bad. He went from green to yellow to red and damn near blue. Nausea was all over him.

"What about me?"

"We'll talk when we get to your place."

"Why can't we talk now?"

"Because I want to concentrate on the road I'm looking out for black ice."Black ice is the icy spots on the road that you cannot see, but you know when you hit it, cause your ass will go sliding all over the highway.

Jay sat there in his seat, quiet as a church mouse. I knew his mind was racing, thinking about what Gerald could have told me. He was already loosing trust in Gerald, but he knew that there was no way under the sun his boy, his main man, his dawg, his friend, would ever stoop so low as to tell me everything that he was doing behind my back, not to mention, all the stuff we talked about privately.

I pulled into the parking space next to Gerald's car.

"I see he finally got that back glass fixed." Jay said, as he stepped out the car.

As we got the luggage out the trunk and walked past Gerald's car, there was a loud scratching sound.

"What was that?" Jay asked, looking around

"I don't know," I replied, as we walked up to the door. Jay acted like he really didn't want to go in. He had the look of a kid that had a fucked up report card and knew the moment he showed his parents, his ass was tore out the frame. That was the look Jay had as he pushed his key into the lock.

Gerald was sitting on the sofa, "Wuz up dawg?" He shouted, as Jay and I walked into the apartment. Gerald didn't even acknowledge me being there. We talked about keeping the appearance that everything is the same as it was before the holiday until it was the right time to tell Jay.

Jay hardly acknowledged the warm welcome, "Can we have some privacy please?"

Gerald just smiled, got up and went into his bedroom without saying another word. As Gerald left the room, I turned and looked Jay directly in his eyes. There was no need in avoiding the inevitable. I was straight to the point

"We can't see each other anymore."

"Why not?" Jay's eyes were as big as baseballs as he tried to understand what I was saying to him.

"I've found somebody else I want to be with."

Jay looked like a kicked puppy as I dismissed him.

"Where the hell is this coming from Destiny? When I left, everything was cool. Why the sudden changes?" Jay was in shock. He walked around the room like a caged animal trying to make sense of it all.

"I've met somebody else, and I want to start kicking it with him.

"Who is he?" Jay stopped walked dead in his tracks. He wanted to know who the man smooth enough to take me away from him was.

"Don't worry about all that. All you need to know is that he's a nigga not afraid to eat pussy!"

"Is that what this is all about? Eatin pussy?"

Jay was frantic. Tears were in his eyes. I walked over to the door and placed my hand on the knob. I was about to walk out the apartment, but I figured I had to get it off of my chest now. He had to know exactly why I was leaving him and how I felt. I was hurt and he was going to know it.

"Don't cry now! Your ass wasn't crying when you were fucking all those other bitches were you?"

"Who told you that? I never fucked around on you!" Jay walked up to me trying to grab my arm.

"Don't touch me muthafucka! Don't worry 'bout who told me. All you need to know is that I'm out. Oh, and keep the jacket, I got it on clearance at Marshalls."

It felt good telling his ass off. Now he's standing here tears all over his face.

"Baby please, let's talk about this. If I did something wrong, let's talk about it. I can explain everything if you let me know what's going on. I don't know who told you what. But, I've never cheated on you. I love you too much!"

I turned around and looked him dead in his eyes

"You have no clue how to love me. And I don't have time to teach a grown ass man how to love and treat a woman. Your mama and daddy should have taught you that."

With that, I walked out the door.

**************************************

I sat on the edge of the bed and listened to Destiny tear Jay a new one. I guess I should feel bad but I don't because he knows the rules we play by. He didn't claim her as his woman, so it's open season on that ass. And since I mentioned ass, I might as well call ole stupid ass Nicole, make up and get her over here to suck my dick. All I had to do was tell her everything, she wanted to hear, and bingo, I'll be up in that pussy once again. I knew she was crazy but I also knew she had good sex.

"Come over tomorrow night and spend the night with me," I told Nicole.

"What time do you want me there?"

"Around 7 o'clock, I wanna start early on that ass." I heard the front door close. I had to get back into the front room to see the damage.

"Hey holla at me tomorrow aiight, round 7 o'clock," I said trying to hurry up and get off the phone.

"OK."

I hung up the phone. "I don't know what it is about crazy ass light skin women but they got the best pussy." I said to myself, as I walked into the front room. As soon as I sat foot in the front room, Jay started.

"What did you and Destiny talk about the other day?" he asked, with a bold stare on his face.

"What are you talking about?"

"While I was out of town," Jay looked me square in the eyes and asked again. "What did you and Destiny talk about? She said y'all talked about me. What did you tell her?"

Not knowing what Destiny had actually said, "We talked about our college days and our childhoods, that's about it, why?" I kept a straight face while telling the half-truth to Jay. The way I saw it, a half-truth was better than a full lie any day.

"She just broke up with me," Jay said with his head down in a whispered voice.

I stood there with a confused look on his face. I did not know she was gonna do all that. I just wanted to sleep with her, I never meant for her to break up with Jay.

"That's fucked up man. Did she say why?"

In a very shaky voice, Jay answered. "All she said is that she was with a new nigga that eat pussy."

"Damn man you wasn't eatlin' the pussy?"

"Hell no, I'm not putting my mouth on anything a female piss out of."

"You like getting your dick sucked right?"

"Yeah."

"So what the fuck do you think is on her mind when she is sucking your dick. You know, the thing you piss out of. I told you a while ago, if you have a woman and you want to keep her satisfied you better eat the pussy; make a meal out of it, put your face in it. Make her feel like you're trying to find your way back to the womb. I told you that before. So now it's a nigga out there and all he had to do was eat her right and she's out. That's your damn fault."

Jay stormed out of the apartment. "I guess the nigga didn't want to hear the truth," I said to myself, as I went into the kitchen to get something to drink and a Pop Tart.

The next morning, I could tell that nigga Jay had not slept at all because of trying to figure out what had happened, why was Destiny's heart set on leaving him. Never being one to not kick a man while he's down, I started in on Jay bright and early.

"So, now I guess you gonna sit around the apartment all day looking like a bitch," I said, sounding disgusted. "Fuck that bitch man. The best way to get over some pussy is to replace it. Get on the phone find another freak and call it a day. "Outta sight, outta mind", is my motto." I don't believe in being in the dumps over NO female. It's too many out there for me to be crying over one. See that's the problem with women today, they think they have the pussy game on lock. But it's not like that at all. I get pussy by the pound, and ain't afraid to let one walk when it's another right behind her wanting the number one spot.

As Jay walked around looking like a kicked dog, there was a knock at the door. I waited for a second to see if he was going to make an attempt to answer it but he was too busy crying in his cereal. I just got up and went to the door. I looked through the peephole and saw Destiny. Not thinking anything of it, I opened the door. "Wuz up?"

"Hey, you ready?" she asked.

"Ready for what?" My face was frowned, trying to figure out what she was talking about. I guess Jay heard her voice, got up from the table, and walked over to the door. Now both of us are standing there looking like dick head of the week.

"I want to spend the day with you. I have our day all planned out."

The look on her face was excitement and she looked extremely happy. She even grabbed my hand and tried to lightly pull me out the door.

For the first time, I was speechless. I just kind stood there with my mouth hung open. Without even looking I could tell Jay was standing next to me ready to explode.

"What the fuck is this about?" Jay asked, starring a hole through my head.

My mouth was still hung open. My brain was scrambling for an answer, but my mouth was getting drier and drier by the second from the fresh air going in.

"Dawg, I, I, I don't know what the hell is going on."

Destiny cut me off, "I want to spend the day with you because it's a lot we have to talk about."

"What the hell do the two of you possibly have to say to each other? Y'all can't stand each other anyway." Jays light complexion was beet red at this point. He could not believe that two people that hated each other as much as the two of us, wanted to spend time to talk.

Destiny stood in the doorway looking very calm.

"Gerald, go put on some clothes so we can go. I'll wait for you in the car." She turned and walked away not saying another word to either of us.

As I walked into my bedroom Jay was right on my heels.

"You fucked her didn't you?" He yelled, as I kept walking, pretending not to hear him. "Nigga, I'm talkin' to you! You fucked her didn't you?"

I am not one to get punched in my house, "No, I didn't fuck her! But if I did, what's the problem? You said y'all weren't serious anyway. Did you or did you not say that? " I turned and was looking Jay directly in his eyes, "Nigga, you know the rules. You didn't claim her so she's open season." I knew that Jay would not try to back me against the wall like that again. "As a matter of fact, since y'all ain't kicking it anymore, I think I will go hang with ole girl, she seems kinda cool."

Jay was furious. He paced around the room as I talked about how cool Destiny was and how much we had in common. If looks could kill I'll be a dead muthafucka right about now.

Suddenly, Jay stopped walking and dropped his head."You right man," Jay said, as if admitting defeat, "I didn't claim her, so it's all good. Besides, no bitch is worth losing your boy over anyway."

Jay walked over to me and extended his hand in friendship. I knew that nigga was a punk, but damn I didn't know he was going to back down like this. If the shoe was on the other foot, I'll still be beating his ass from last night. That nigga head would be swollen for a year. I extended my hand and we embraced. I guess he called himself forgiving me and I could have cared less. But, I couldn't just crush his manhood totally. "Bitches ain't shit man, you know that?" I said, as I walked out my room after getting dressed.

Jay never said another word, as I walked towards the door. I looked back at Jay, "Don't worry man. I'll tell you every word she says."I walked out the door and saw Destiny sitting in her car, talking on the phone. She was laughing like she had just heard the funniest joke this century. I stared at her as I walked up to the car. I'm pretty good at reading lips and could have sworn she said to whomever she was talking to, something about fuck his best friend.

I got in the car and instantly questioned Destiny, "What the hell are you doing?"

"What do you mean?"

"Why did you just do that?"

"What are you..."

I cut her off, "Stop trippin' Destiny. What was that all about?"

"Like I told y'all in the house, I really want to talk and hang out with you today."

It looked really suspicious but I went along with it. After all, Destiny was fine and we had already taken a bite out of the forbidden fruit.

\*\*\*\*\*\*\*\*\*\*\*\*\*\*\*\*\*\*\*\*\*\*\*\*\*\*\*\*\*\*\*\*\*\*\*\*\*\*\*

Destiny's plan was working spectacular. Jay sat in the apartment and almost drove himself crazy.

"What are they doing?" Jay asked himself over and over again.

"I know that nigga told her everything I was doing" The more he thought about It, the more upset he got.

He walked around in circles in the apartment. Part of him wanted to go out and look for them, the other part of him wanted to wait outside in the bushes and creep Gerald and Destiny as they walked back into the apartment. He had broken out in a cold sweat and was starting to shake uncontrollably. The only thing that stopped him from going completely over the edge, was someone had started knocking on the door.

Jay got up to answer the door. "Who is it?" he barked.

"Nicole.".

Jay opened the door, "He ain't here!"

"Well, hello to you too!" She said, with a serious attitude.

"My bad, wuz up Nicole...he ain't here."

"Where is he?"

Jay looked at Nicole and figured out the perfect way to take a stab at Gerald.

"He's out with his girl."

Nicole's face turned into an instant frown.

"What the hell do you mean he's out with his girl?"

Jay noticed that Nicole had an overnight bag with her, "They left for the weekend"

You could almost see the anger as it rose from her feet to the top of her head.

"How the fuck is he gonna ask me to stay the night with him and his ass is out of town with another bitch?"

Gerald had told Jay on several occasions that Nicole was crazy as hell and had a short fuse and Jay lit it. Talk about shit just falling in your lap. He would let Nicole get Gerald, that way his hands didn't get dirty.

All he had to do was throw fuel on the flame.

"He said something about you coming over and given me some if he wasn't here."

You could see the fire in her eyes as Jay spoke.

"No the fuck he didn't say that. This ain't pass the pussy. I don't get down like that."

Nicole walked around like a caged animal. She turned to Jay

"I tell you what, I'm gonna leave him a note in his room so he know I stopped by."

She picked up her bag, walked into his room and began to thumb tack her thongs on his wall. She laid her bra on his pillow and her black teddy over his television. She went into her bag and pulled out a tube of red lipstick.

I hope you and your bitch had a wonderful weekend, she wrote on his dresser mirror. Jay stood to the bedroom door and watched as Nicole had her way with Gerald's room.

This was the best Jay felt all day. He felt like the scales of justice had tilted in his favor. He almost felt liberated.

"I guess every dog has his day," he said to Nicole, as she left the apartment.

He closed the door behind Nicole and went back and closed Gerald's door. Nicole hadn't been gone a good thirty minutes before Destiny and Gerald pulled up into the parking lot.

***********************************

Destiny parked next to Gerald's car.

"What the fuck is that?" I yelled, as I got out of the car. "Somebody scratched the hell out of my car... it had to happen recently cause that was not there when I got the back glass fixed." I walked around the car cursing to the top of my lungs. I looked at my watch and realized it was 9:45pm.

"Damn, I forgot!" I yelled.

"Forgot what baby?"

"Nothing, don't worry about it."

As the two of us walked into the apartment Destiny made sure to hug me. I knew she was hoping that Jay was looking.

"What's goin' on Dawg?" I asked, as I made my way to my room.

"Not a thing, just sitting here chilaxin."

Destiny sat on the sofa across from Jay, trying not to look at him.

I opened my door and turned on my light. "What the fuck happened in here?"

Destiny jumped up to see what the problem was. I turned around and saw Destiny and Jay walking fast towards me.

"Um, you have to go. I have a personal matter I need to take care of." I said to Destiny, walking her to the front door.

"What's wrong?" She asked, as I tried to push her out the door.

"I'll tell you later. Have a good night." I closed the door and ran back to my room.

"Jay why didn't you call me and tell me that bitch Nicole was over here?"

"Dawg it happened so fast I didn't think about it."

"Why did you let her in my room?"

"Like I said man, she asked where you were, I told her I didn't know, she walked in your room, and walked out the house just like that."

It took everything in me not to beat his ass on the spot. We are supposed to be friends and he let this shit happen. See, this is why I don't trust niggas!

"You had to tell her, cause she wrote I hope you and your bitch had a great weekend on my mirror."

Jay looked like he wanted to laugh a little but he knew if he did I was going to be all over his ass in a matter of seconds.

"I told her you were gone for the weekend. I didn't say with who or where you went. I was trying to cover for you."

I was mad enough to spit fire.

"I catch her ass in the street, I'm gonna beat her like she's a man!" I screamed, as I snatched her nasty, caked up thongs off the wall.

I laid across the bed. After a few seconds of lying there I started to sniff the air, then sniff my comforter.

"Damn, and she sprayed my comforter with her funky ass perfume."

Neither Gerald nor Jay said more than two words to each other since the day Destiny came over and took Gerald out a week ago. Destiny made it a point to come over every day to hang out with Gerald, making Jay's life a living hell. Today would be different. Today she finally put the final part of her plan in action.

Gerald and Destiny sat on the sofa watching T.V. as Jay tried to act like everything was cool. Every so often, Destiny would cuddle up next to Gerald and he would kinda nudge her back across the sofa. It ate Jay up that the girl he wanted was now seeing his so called friend. She would look over at him from time to time and he wouldn't give her the satisfaction of looking in her direction. Jay sat in the chair across from them and tried to watch television as if everything was normal. He had one split second of weakness and looked over at Destiny and that was all she needed.

"Gerald, can we go in your room? I want to ask you something," Gerald, never really feeling comfortable about spending time in the house with Destiny while Jay was there, got up and walked towards the room. As Gerald walked past Destiny to go to the room, she added a small jab to Jay's ribs.

"Damn that nigga fine," she whispered to herself, but loud enough for Jay to hear.

Gerald sat on the bed and waited for Destiny to come through the door.

"Wuz up?" Gerald asked, as Destiny walked slowly towards him.

"I'm gonna be straight forward. I'm horny as hell"

Gerald's eyes grew to the size of baseballs. As much as he liked to fuck, even he knew this was crossing a dangerous line.

"But your boy... I mean Jay, is in the front room," he said in a frantic whisper.

"And?"

It was obvious that she was out to hurt Jay, but Gerald was weak when it came to having sex. When pussy called, Gerald was sure to answer. Reluctantly and with a deep and loud exhale of breath, he finally spoke up after sitting there looking like a mischievous child

"Aiight, but you gotta be quiet."

Destiny looked at him with a yeah right look on her face. Gerald walked over to the television and turned the volume up a bit to drown out any escaping sounds. He pulled her away from the door to the other side of the room. He wanted to make sure that she was far away from Jay as possible. He even turned the radio up just in case she decided to make it known what they we doing.

Gerald grabbed her hips and pulled her close. She wrapped her arms around his neck and leaned forward for a kiss.

Gerald ran his tongue around her lips. They licked each other's tongue at the same time as the temperature in the room was starting to heat up. She pulled his shirt over his head revealing his hairy well-developed chest.

"Damn, I love a hairy man" Destiny said as she worked her way down to suck his nipples. Gerald stood there with his manhood growing larger and thicker with every suck and nibble. Grabbing his dick and feeling that it was almost at maximum length, she unzipped his pants and began to gently bite on his dick while he was still wearing his boxer briefs. Gerald was the type of guy that liked a small amount of pain during sex, so this turned him on tremendously. He caught himself moaning rather loud and pulled back a little. Destiny, realizing what he was doing, snatched down his boxer-briefs. To her surprise, Gerald had shaved off all of his pubic hair. This made his dick look another two inches longer. She began to suck his dick as if her life depended on it. She made slurping sounds as if she was getting that last bit of soda out of a bottle with a straw. She used a lot of spit, letting it fall from her mouth and land on his legs and her shirt.

Gerald was getting really into it and started moaning and talking to her while she performed.

"That's right boo, suck my dick. You like that shit don't you?"

He no longer cared if Jay heard him. In fact, Jay did hear him and walked towards the bedroom door. He stood outside the door and could barely hear Gerald talking over the noise of the TV and radio.

"Squeeze my balls while you suck me," he demanded, and Destiny obliged with every command. She only stopped sucking his dick long enough to snatch her shirt off and toss it on the floor next to her. She let go of his balls, took her hand, reached between his legs, and slapped him on the ass.

Jay wanted to run in the room and beat the hell out of both of them, but he figured his time was coming. So he just stood there and listened, getting madder and madder with every passing second.

Gerald was so turned on from all the things Destiny was doing, he finally decided to return the favor. He pulled her up by the shoulders and tossed her on the bed. The biggest smile ran across her face as he roughly pulled off her pants and panties. He dived face first into her pussy with a fury, licking everywhere. The mixture of her wetness and his saliva drove her crazy. He nibbled on her clit driving her wild. She was moaning and screaming as he gave her head. He pulled his lips away from her pussy, removed her satisfaction from his face with his hand, and licked his fingers clean.

"How does my pussy taste?" she asked, looking him in the face. He answered by holding her pussy lips apart, fully extending his tongue and sticking it as far into her as he could. She grabbed his head and forcefully held his face in that position.

"That's it nigga, eat Mamma pussy"

He pushed her knees towards her shoulders exposing her ass hole. He licked her ass, making her beg for more. He stuck his tongue in her ass and fucked her with it. He took two fingers and moved them around in Destiny's pussy getting them nice and wet. Gerald then slowly pushed those two fingers into her ass as he ate her out. She cried out with pure delight as he did this. Her breathing became short and almost asthma sounding. Her heart felt as if it was about to jump out of her chest. She once again grabbed his head and came all over his face.

Jay was sitting back on the sofa and heard all the sounds coming out of the room, even though the television in the front room and in Gerald's bedroom was loud.

"How could my boy do me like that?" he asked himself. "That nigga suppose to be my boy. That's aiight, enjoy it now nigga. I'll have the last laugh, believe that". Jay sat on the sofa with a very disturbed look on his face. The more noise they made in the bedroom, the more pissed off Jay became. The next sound he heard really drove him crazy. It was the sound of the box spring on Gerald's bed started to squeak from two bodies lying on it.

Gerald climbed on top of Destiny and slammed his dick into her rough and hard. She screamed with every thrust of his thick dick. The harder he fucked her, the louder she became. The bed sounded if it was going to fall to pieces. The headboard banged against the wall. After a few minutes of headboard banging sex they change positions. He laid her on her side, lift one of her legs in the air and the other flat on the bed. He was able to fuck her pussy and feel her ass on his dick at the same time.

"Fuck me nigga!" She screamed, as he continued to pound her.

The sex was very rough just the way they both liked it. He put her on her hands and knees and fucked her from the back.

Grabbing a hand full of her hair and yanking her head backwards, he plowed into her like a jackhammer.

"Spank me daddy," she screamed, demanding to have her ass smacked.

Jay stormed out of the apartment. He could not take it anymore.

"That nigga aint shit!" he said, as he walked around the complex. Every thought he had was of hurting Gerald. People that lived in the complex watched as he walked around looking like a mad man.

Back in the apartment, Gerald felt himself ready to cum, but it was feeling too good to stop. They both knew he was not wearing any protection and she was not on the pill. Lust had a grip on them and they could not get loose. Part of Gerald wanted to stop before he came. He even thought about pulling out right before he was ready to cum and shoot off all over her. But her warm wet pussy felt so good around his dick. Without thinking about it, he shot wad after wad of cum deep into her. Destiny wanted to get back at Jay, but she knew she had taken it too far. She was caught up in the moment of feeling good and totally lost her mind. One thing she prided herself on, was not getting pregnant till she wanted to get pregnant. She had been with several men and never once let one of them get near her without a condom on. Getting Jay back for what he had done to her was one thing, but letting Gerald cum in her was something she had not anticipated happening. After he came they both just laid in the bed motionless and silent. She laid with her back to him and he laid flat on his back staring at the ceiling. They both wanted to say something but they both knew they had crossed a line that never should have been crossed. Gerald broke the silence first.

"You know, I can't have kids. The doctor said I have a low sperm count."

Destiny rolling over on her stomach
"Shut the hell up."

She was angry as hell but not at Gerald. More at herself for letting the situation get like this. She looked at Gerald and smiled, "I guess it's a waiting game now."

"Yeah, I guess so."

Even though Gerald was a tough guy on the outside, it was always one person that could get to him, his mother.

"Guess who I ran into today?" Gerald's mother was always running into an old friend of his.

"Who this time, ma?"

"Dawn," the phone went silent for a second, "She said it's been almost 6 months since she last saw you."

"Did you give her my number?" Gerald asked, trying not to sound too excited. Dawn was a very thin, caramel complexion young woman that Gerald was crazy over in college. The two of them were inseparable when they were dating.

"Yes I did. I figured that y'all were such an item in school, that it might do you some good, since you're alone up there."

Gerald laughed a little, knowing that his mother didn't know her son was running through women like a hooker through condoms.

"We didn't end on a good note at all."

Gerald's mother was the type of mom that no matter what you said or wanted, she always knew what was best for you.

"Well y'all have both grown up a little and no sense in holding a grudge."

"We'll see."

Gerald sat around the rest of the day thinking about Dawn. I swear mama need to mind her business sometimes, he said to himself as he thought about all the good times they had in college. Dawn, Jay and Gerald all hung out together. Dawn and Gerald was the couple, and Jay was kinda the third wheel, but they made him feel like they were just one small family.

Jay walked into the room still not really saying too much to Gerald.

"Jay, guess who ma dukes ran into today?"

"Who?" Jay answered, very nonchalantly

"Dawn"

Instantly a small smile ran across Jay's face.

"For real?" Jay asked, as he started thinking about the night all hell broke loose back in Miami.

"My mama said she gave her the number so she might be calling."

Jay walked away laughing to himself thinking, "Shit bout to hit the fan again."

\*\*\*\*\*\*\*\*\*\*\*\*\*\*\*\*\*\*\*\*\*\*\*\*\*\*\*\*\*\*\*\*\*\*\*\*\*\*\*\*

Six months ago: July 4th Miami, Florida can only mean one thing...it is hot, hot as hell. Everybody is wearing a lot of nothing and hormones are running wild on college campuses from the south campus of the University of Miami, to the north campus of F.I.U.

With the sun blazing, the music up load, and the women damn near naked; life was good, damn good. This was no day to be sitting inside watching TV.

"You going to the beach with us today, right?" Gerald asked Jay, walking from dormitory to dormitory trying to find all the fellas so they could hit the road.

"Dawn going?" Jay replied

"Nah, she's going to help one of her girl friends move into her apartment today."

Jay looked at Gerald with excitement in his eyes

"That means, let's get them hoes, man!"

All the fellas jumped in Gerald car and they hit the road; Biscayne Blvd to McArthur Causeway, Next stop, sand, sun and ass; better known as South Beach.

Bikinis and thongs were all you could see at the beach. Every shape ass you could want to see was out; the big bouncy ass, the small tight ass, the ass with lumps in it. The ass that was so flat you could still see the thong string in the middle of it; it was all out there.

Jay announced "Well fellas, this is the last time we'll be on the beach as college kids. It's time to find hoes, hoes and mo hoes!"

There were woman walking around with what looked like dental floss on. One young lady had on a two-piece thong set that left nothing to the imagination. With the sun beating down on South Beach and the ocean spray hitting you in the face, you knew this was the perfect weather for a young man's dreams to come true. Nevertheless, Gerald was not interested in any of these women. The woman that he desired was not there.

"Dawg, will you loosen up and holla at some of these women."

Jay grew tired of looking at Gerald walk around trying not to notice all the beautiful women along the beach.

"What the hell is wrong wit you. You all depressed; looking like a lost puppy. Nigga its pussy by the pound out here and you all upset because one pussy is not here. Outta site, outta mind is what you always say right?"

\*\*\*\*\*\*\*\*\*\*\*\*\*\*\*\*\*\*\*\*\*\*\*\*\*\*\*\*\*\*\*\*\*\*\*\*\*\*\*

At the apartment: Both Gerald and Jay sat in the front room trying not to look at one another. Jay wanted to get up and stick a knife right into Gerald's neck. Just sitting in the same room with Gerald drove him crazy.

The telephone rang and since Gerald's name was on the bill Jay made sure he only answered it when he knew someone was calling for him.

Gerald answered the phone.

"May I speak to Gerald please?"

Gerald recognized the voice on the other end on the phone. His face went from stern to smiling.

"Wuz up, Dawn?" He didn't want to sound excited or upset that she called.

"I see your mother told you I saw her today."

"Yeah, she told me. So, how have you been?" Gerald was hoping that Dawn was in a relationship with the man of her dreams.

"I'm good, working like a slave but it's all good. And you?"

He wanted to tell her that he owned his own company and making millions, but he knew she would see right through that. She always knew when he was lying. He wanted to tell her something to let her know he was doing fine and had moved on. "I'm a chef at a very popular hotel." She didn't need to know that he was a nighttime line cook. Gerald took over the conversation, "So what do you want? It's been six months since we last spoke and it can be another six before we speak again. I sat by the phone that night waiting on you to call me and explain your actions, but you never did."

Raising his voice, "And what's really fucked up is, you were the one that did the wrong. And I was sitting and waiting. So what do you possibly want to say to me now?"

Dawn sat on the other end "You done" she asked sarcastically.

"I wanted to call you a long time ago, but Jay said it was not a good idea for me to talk to you. Every time I saw you in the street, you just walked past me like I wasn't there."

Her voice sounded like a woman begging for forgiveness. "I know I was foul for what I did, but you have to understand that at the time we were all young and stupid. We all did things we wish we could take back."

Gerald didn't know what to say. He held the phone wondering if he should curse her out some more or to tell her that he always kept a spot in his heart for her.

"That's bullshit! You knew damn well how I felt and that shit didn't mean a thing to you!"

The Gerald that she knew in college was not the same Gerald now.

"You taught me a lesson back then Dawn. I now know what I will and will not accept from women!"

\*\*\*\*\*\*\*\*\*\*\*\*\*\*\*\*\*\*\*\*\*\*\*\*\*\*\*\*\*\*\*\*\*\*\*\*\*\*\*\*

As night fell over Miami, Gerald had not heard from Dawn all day.

"We are going to Coco Walk tonight. I know you rolling or are you sitting here on the porch waitin for Massa to come up the trail." Jay said in an old slave voice.

"I'll roll. Let's go."

On the way to Coco Walk, Gerald called Dawn's cell phone repeatedly.

"Where the hell is she?" he thought to himself.

Jay looked over at Gerald in the passenger seat, "I know the pussy ain't that good. Nigga we used to run trains on bitches remember. We fucked from sun up to sundown. No female was out our league."

Jay was trying to get Gerald to be his old self and stop worrying about one woman. "Listen to me man. It is not meant for one man to have one woman. You know why?"

Gerald looked at Jay with a "what the fuck are you talking about" look, "Because one woman is not enough for one man. If God meant for one man to be with one woman, he would not have made titties and asses' different sizes. He's giving us a choice and who am I to look a gift horse in the mouth. In other words, let's line 'em up and knock 'em down tonight."

Gerald couldn't help but laugh at that stupid bit of knowledge Jay was trying to teach him.

\*\*\*\*\*\*\*\*\*\*\*\*\*\*\*\*\*\*\*\*\*\*\*\*\*\*\*\*\*\*\*\*\*\*\*\*\*\*

"Gerald, I never meant to hurt you," Dawn was trying to plead her case. "I made a mistake and I've been paying for it since that night." Gerald's eyes were blood red with anger. "Your mom told me that you were alone up there and it might do you some good to see a friendly face."

"Jay is up here also. We live together now. So if I need a friendly face I'll look at his." Right then, Jay shot Gerald the nastiest look he could muster.

Jay listened as Gerald talked to Dawn. He remembered how crazy Gerald was about her. He remembered how every time they all went out Gerald couldn't have a good time for worrying about if Dawn was having a good time.

Then it hit him, "She was my friend too and I think now is a better time than any to see an old familiar face."

"Dawg, what are you getting into tonight?" Jay asked, as he and Gerald called themselves cleaning up.

"Nada tonight, just chillin." Jay walked over to Gerald wanting to whip his ass on the spot, but he was picking his time.

"Call Destiny over, I want to introduce her to my new girl." Gerald looking stunned, kinda smirked at Jay

"What new girl?"

"Y'all will meet her tonight."

"What she look like?" Gerald asked, as he sat up from slumping down in the sofa.

"She straight, like I said y'all will meet her tonight. It's a big surprise."

Gerald turned towards the television not paying Jay any mind. Jay was bubbling over with so much excitement; it was hard for him to contain himself knowing what he had planned.

Gerald walked into his room and picked up the phone to call Destiny. "Your boy wants me to invite you over tonight to meet his new girl."

"Why the hell would I want to do that," Destiny asked, with irritation in her voice.

"I don't know. He's all happy, acting giddy."

"Fine, I'll come around there. I don't care, maybe with his new girl he'll stop looking at me all funny." Destiny hung up the phone and laid back on her bed. "Well since he's introducing a new woman tonight, I might as well drop my own little bomb.

Around 7 p.m., Destiny showed up at the apartment looking fine as ever. She wanted to look her best since she was meeting Jay's new girl. Destiny wanted Jay to see what he was no longer getting. She wore a tan Cashmere sweater, tight fitting Girbaud Jeans and her favorite pair of tan pumps. She was stepping in style and knew that this new woman would have to bring it, in order to out shine her this night. As she walked into the apartment, both Gerald and Jay stood and stared as she walked over to the sofa and sat down.

"What y'all staring at?"

Gerald sat next to her "Damn girl, you banging tonight, what's the occasion?"

"I have a surprise for you later. "

"What is it?"

"I'll tell you later"

Jay knowing that Destiny would try to outdo his surprise did not give her the pleasure by saying anything about the way she looked. He just smiled and walked into the kitchen.

"Has he said anything to you about his girl?" Destiny asked Gerald.

"All he told me was that we would meet her tonight. He didn't say anything else about it."

Ten minutes later, there was a knock at the door. Jay ran from the kitchen to open the door. When the door opened, it seemed like the air had been sucked from Gerald's lungs. He sat on the sofa eyes as big as quarters and mouth dropped open. Jay broke the silence.

"Dawn, wuz up girl?" Jay hugged her and looked back at Gerald. The look on Gerald's face was pure shock, and Jay was just getting started.

"Damn, you look good."

"Thank you, what's going on with you? It's been a little while."

"You know me, chillin as always."

She turned her head and looked at Gerald, who was still sitting there with a blank stare.

"How are you Gerald?" Dawn asked, in a very seductive voice.

Gerald sat there for a second or two before answering.

"I'm good, and you?"

"Great, since I get to see you again."

Destiny sat next to Gerald wondering what was going on. She was under the impression that Gerald did not know this woman. However, it was obvious that the two of them had a history.

"Hello, I'm Destiny," she said in a very bold tone, breaking the stare between Dawn and Gerald.

"Hi, I'm Dawn, an old friend of Gerald's."

"And Jay's!" Gerald quickly pointed out.

"It's always nice to meet my man's old friends." Destiny was very straightforward with her words, letting Dawn know that Gerald was spoken for.

"Your man? Gerald, you didn't mention that you had a girlfriend."

"Didn't know I needed to last we spoke," Gerald was furious. Destiny was very upset at this point but was not trying to show it.

"From our last conversation, I thought I made it clear that I had moved on!" anger was flowing through Gerald's veins. "Besides, what the hell are you doing here anyway?"

"To be honest, I was invited to come up here."

Jay saw this as the perfect opportunity to step in and throw another dagger at his friend.

"Yeah dawg, I thought it would be nice to see her again, so I invited her."

"So this was your surprise for everybody? Invite my ex for a visit!"

Destiny's head turned sharply toward Gerald, "Your ex! What the fuck kind of games are y'all playing?" Destiny was infuriated with the position she was put in. "You have me come the fuck over here to meet your ex, that's fucked up Gerald!"

Jay, smiling the entire time Destiny went on her tirade, soaked up the fact that Gerald was stuck between a rock and a hard place with two women.

Dawn tried to defuse the situation, "It was a long time ago."

"Shut the fuck up! You come strolling your narrow ass up in here starting shit!" Destiny was losing her composure, all the things that she thought made up the perfect lady was out the window.

"Calm down. Jay invited her. I didn't know she was coming up here," Gerald pleaded. At that point Gerald caught himself explaining his actions. "Wait a minute, who the fuck are you to be cursing people in my house? You wanna curse somebody do it from the other side of the door! I told you I had nothing to do with this but you still coming at me like this is my fault. Either calm down, or bounce!"

"Fuck you, I'm out!" Destiny stood and walked towards the door.

Gerald snatched open the door, "Bye!"

"Fuck you nigga!"

Gerald slammed the door behind her as she stormed past him. Jay and Dawn sat on the sofa looking like they had nothing to do with what had just transpired. Destiny had forgotten all about her surprise she had for Gerald, as she drove off mad at the world.

"You ain't shit ole bitch ass nigga!" Gerald screamed at Jay, looking as if he wanted to jump on him.

"Don't get mad at me cause your bitch crazy"

Gerald walked into his room and slammed the door. Jay and Dawn sat on the sofa and laughed about the entire situation. They both got what they wanted. Jay had Gerald and Destiny fighting and Dawn had Gerald to herself for the few days she would be in town. Jay looked over at Dawn, "Damn that could not have worked out more perfect if we had planned it that way. Oh wait a second, we did!" They both laughed and continued to catch up on old times.

The next morning Gerald awoke before anybody else in the house. He sat on the edge of the bed, stretched and scratched his balls. "Damn I hope last night was just a bad dream." He stood to his bedroom doorway hoping that when he walked out the room only Jay would be laying on the sofa snoring and farting as normal. As he walked into the front room he saw Jay first, laying on the floor in the fetal position, wrapped up in his comforter. "I should kick the shit out of his punk ass for that fucked up dream I had last night," Gerald said between clenched teeth. He turned and looked at the sofa and saw Dawn. "Damn that shit wasn't a dream," he said as he saw her lying on the sofa with one of her well-toned light skin legs hanging out from under her cover.

His eyes strolled slowly up her leg and stopped on her small round behind that was sitting up like a ripe peach under her sheets. Gerald looked at the two of them for a few seconds wondering if he should wake them up and tell both of them to get the hell out of his apartment or just let what happened last night go.

"Wake the fuck up!" he screamed to the top of his lungs. Jay and Dawn both shook with surprise as he screamed at them. Jay scrambled around on the floor like he was drowning in a pool of water. Dawn damn near fell off the sofa as she jumped from the sudden screams in the apartment.

"Both of y'all pack yo shit and bounce!"

Jay was the first to speak, "What the fuck is wrong with you? Who the fuck is you to come up in here yelling at people?"

Dawn sat up on the sofa, whipping the sleep from her eyes trying to figure out what all the yelling was about. "What are you two screaming for?"

Gerald was shaking with anger, "Both of y'all get up and get out," he said trying to sound as calm as possible. "My name is the only one on the lease, so I'm the only one staying."

"I paid my half of the rent for this month, so I ain't going no fucking where!" Jay said, with a harsh and bold tone in his voice.

Jay felt this was as good a time as any to finally let Gerald know how he felt over the last few months. "I have put up with your shit for too long Gerald. I've had you lie on me, talk to me any kinda way, and steal my girl. Enough of this shit is enough!" Jay was standing toe to toe with Gerald. Both men looked like they were ready to kill on command.

"Then leave nigga!" Gerald said in a high pitched almost screaming tone. "If you're not happy hear leave. Take your ass back to Florida. I didn't want you up here with me in the first fucking place."

Jay decided to take a shot at Gerald's ego.

"We were supposed to move up here together, but you were too busy running from Dawn and left before I did."

Dawn looked up bewildered, "What do you mean running from me?"

It was finally time for Gerald to face Dawn and tell her why he left. He rounded on Dawn and was now looking directly in her light brown eyes.

"That night at Coco Walk in the club. We saw you dancing, oh, my bad, damn near fucking some bitch on the dance floor. Imagine how I felt standing there with all my boys and my girl is on the floor rubbing and squeezing some female titties. Then to make matters worse, another dude walked up and y'all tag teamed him. She was all over his dick and you were all over his ass. What was I suppose to do. What was I suppose to think?"

Dawn stood still trying to come up with something to say, but Gerald was far from finished with her.

"I tried to call you all that day; no answer. I didn't even want to go to the club that night, but your boy here made me go. Then to find out that he knew you were going to be at the club that night, I was so mad at him for setting me up to see you like that. I loved you more than anything. I've never loved a woman like I loved you, and you took that and walked all over it like I didn't mean a damn thing to you!"

Dawn just jumped in and interrupted Gerald as he spoke. "I was just enjoying life that night. It meant nothing to me. I was just experimenting with my sexuality and I took it too far. I didn't know I had a thing for women till that day. As for earlier that day, I went to help my girlfriend move. The girl at the club was at the house also and we just clicked. I didn't know how you would react, so I didn't bother to tell you. But, I never thought you would be in the same club as me that night. I mentioned it to Jay, but I didn't know he would take you there to catch me doing something wrong," Dawn explained, while giving Jay the evil eye.

"So this was some shit you were gonna do behind my back then right?" he asked, walking around the room looking half mad, half hurt.

"I didn't know how to tell you." Dawn lowered her head and tried her best to squeeze a few tears out of her eyes.

"What's wrong with telling a brotha that you want to eat some pussy. Shit, we could have worked it out to where all of us could have got together if it meant that much to you."

Dawn opened her mouth to say something and Gerald cut her off before she could say a word.

"What bout ole boy at the club?"

"He was her boyfriend, after that night I never saw either of them again."

Jay watched as the two of them went back and forth. His plan was coming together right in front of him. At this point, he could care less that Gerald still held a grudge from that night. He was just trying to do his boy a favor, so he could stop acting like a love sick puppy.

Gerald didn't know what to say after he heard Dawn's explanation. The room fell silent the only noise was the traffic on the street outside. Dawn broke the silence with a question of her own for Gerald.

"Why didn't you talk to me after that night? You never spoke to me again till the other day when I called up here. You never gave me a chance to explain myself, you just up and left."

Gerald face went from anger to disbelief. His eyes widened and his mouth fell open.

"You didn't bother to explain to me that you were fucking women. You didn't explain to me that you were into anything other than me. So don't try and flip this shit on me, cause I ain't having it. Besides, you weren't going to tell me anyway."

"You're right I wouldn't have told you because it was nothing."

At that point anger swelled inside Gerald and he had heard enough, "It was nothing? Maybe to you it was nothing but to me it was everything. You're half the reason I left, you're the reason I will never give my heart to another woman." Gerald felt like since he was telling folk off, he might as well keep it going and move on to Jay.

"As a matter of fact Jay, you're the reason I'm fucking Destiny. You are the one told me all your business. You're the one who fuck and tell. You've always been like that. Why you think all the boys fucked your women? You made it easy for them. Hell, everybody knew that but your silly ass! All that running around with you in the past is what made me the playa I am. So I guess I owe you a thank you. Plus, I owed you for that shit you pulled in Miami."

Jay wanted to jump on Gerald and beat him near death. He sat there and endured the entire verbal lashing because he knew it was all true.

Gerald continued, "Thank you for making it easy for me to get with Destiny, and you know what, I told the both of you a lie a moment ago. I said that I would never give my heart to another woman. Well I'm a try my best to give it to Destiny. She's a real woman. A woman that I know will be straight up with me, a woman that will always have my back."

Jay's face scowled as his plan just went out the window. The plan was to bring Dawn to Greensboro to win Gerald back. This would cause Destiny and Gerald to break up and he could get back with her. Dawn walked over to Gerald and wrapped her arms around him.

"Get off me, we're done; never again will I give you the opportunity to hurt me."

Dawn ran her right hand over Gerald's cheek. As if she was whipping away a tear. Gerald grabbed her wrist and squeezed tight. He looked her right in her eyes. "Like I said before, pack ya shit and bounce."

Normally Dawn would just bat her eyes at Gerald and he would fold like a bad hand of poker. But today was different, and from the look Gerald had in his eyes, Dawn knew it.

"Can I at least stay for a few more hours? My plane doesn't leave till later tonight."

"Look like you got a long ass wait at the airport then huh?"

"Can I at least brush my teeth before I go? You know, freshen up a bit?"

"Yeah, go ahead but make it quick. The faster your ass can get the hell out of here, the better."

Dawn went into the bathroom to freshen up. Jay and Gerald stood face-to-face hatred was on both their faces. Tension filled the room.

"At the end of the month dawg, your ass is out." If there was ever a time when Gerald meant what he said and said what he meant, that was it. "Just so we are clear. I fucking hate everything about you. Why we've been friends this long is beyond me. I'm tired of you always riding my coattail. I'm tired of looking at you right about now." With that Gerald walked into his bedroom and closed the door so he could call Destiny.

Jay was livid. Everything he wanted he was not going to get this day. He needed to do something to show Destiny that he was the one that really loved her. He had to do something and it had to be done fast.

Gerald knew that he had said some things to Destiny the night before that he knew would hurt her, but he got so caught up in being an ass, he let the one woman that he started having real feelings for walk right out of his house pissed off. He beat himself up mentally for letting her leave the way she did.

When he called her house, she saw his number on the caller ID and wouldn't bother to answer the phone. He called her several times from his house and cell phone, not once did she answer. He went to his neighbor's house and used the phone since Destiny wouldn't recognize that number. She picked up on the first ring.

"Destiny we need to talk."

"'Bout what?" she answered, with the nastiest tone in her voice.

"Come on now, let's not act like that. Let me take you to lunch. I have something I need to say to you face to face."

Sucking her teeth she fired back sounding like a woman scorned. "It's a few things I want to tell you face to face. So yeah, come on and pick me up in about an hour."

With that, she slammed down the phone. Gerald damn near jumped out of his skin when the phone hit the receiver.

He knew this was a one shot deal with Destiny. He realized after throwing Dawn out of his apartment, that he really cared for Destiny. He knew she would have her guard up when she saw him so he figured he'd show up with a little something for her. He purchased a Waterford Crystal long stem rose from Reed's Jewelers. Gerald was not the type to spend more than $20.00 on a gift for a woman. He always figured that the fucking that he gave women was gift enough. But he knew Destiny was different and just breaking her off was not nearly enough for her.

When he arrived at her apartment he didn't know what to expect so he just started talking when she opened the door.

"Look baby, I know I was wrong for the way I handled that situation last night, but I was caught off guard just like you were." The nonchalant look on Destiny's face, made Gerald's nerves worst than they already were. He stumbled over his words and fidgeted his fingers the entire time he talked to her. "I didn't know Jay had invited her up here. Do you think for a second that I would have the woman that I love in the same room with an insignificant ex?"

Destiny's face went from a nonchalant look to confusion all in a second. "What do you mean, the woman that you love?"

"That's right, I love you. I just hate that it took all of this drama before I figured it out." Right then Gerald pulled a long gift wrapped box from his coat and gave it to Destiny.

"What's this?"

"Open it; I got it for you today"

She opened the box and her eyes gazed upon the crystal rose with disbelief. Tears ran down her face because she knew in her heart that Gerald was serious and being very sincere. "Oh my God, Gerald it's beautiful," The front of her blouse was soaked with tears of joy as she took the rose from the box. Nobody has ever given me anything like this before. She thought to herself. "This is a far cry from that fuckin family tree book Jay sorry ass gave me." She said crying while laughing a little.

Gerald was even feeling a little misty "The reason I picked a crystal rose to give you is because it's very fragile like the love I have for you. I've learned to be gentle with your feelings, as well as your heart."

Destiny wrapped her arms around his neck and held on tight. "I love you too baby, I love you too." She whispered in his ear as the two of them embraced and cried together.

For the first time in a while, Gerald felt love again. Destiny was not one of the hoochies that Gerald had met and slept with, without even knowing their name. Destiny was different; totally different.

"I tell you what let's celebrate. Instead of going to lunch, why don't we go take some professional pictures at the mall and just spend quality time together? Not really doing anything in particular, just spend time together."

"That's sounds cool to me baby."

Destiny walked into her bedroom to get ready to leave and looked in the mirror. "I have to tell him today. There is no way I can let another day go by without him knowing the truth." She said softly to herself, almost hating the person that was looking back at her.

Just then, she heard Gerald calling her name, "Hey baby let's just meet at the mall. I have to make a few stops. I'll just meet you at the photo place in about an hour, alright?"

"Yeah that's cool I have to finish getting dressed anyway."

As Gerald left her apartment, Destiny knew tonight was the night she would tell Gerald her secret she's been holding on to. She was excited and happy everything she ever wanted was coming true. But, she was saddened at not knowing what the end of the day had in store for her new relationship.

When Gerald got back to his place after leaving Destiny's apartment, he noticed that Dawn had left. Jay was sitting on the sofa watching television. The two men still had a little to settle between them.

"Gerald man we need to talk, I think we both said some foul shit to each other today and I want to squash this beef between us."

Gerald looked at Jay with a smile, "I don't have a beef with you dawg. I spoke my peace on it earlier, now I'm done with it."

Jay's face looked as if his best friend was back and all was well with the world. "So you still want me out at the end of the month?" He asked laughing, because he knew the answer was going to be no. Jay and Gerald have had fights before and Gerald has always backed off his threats, so why would this time be any different?

"The sooner the better," Gerald answered, sounding calm and collected.

"After all we've been through it's gonna end like this! I had your back when nobody else did. It was me that exposed Dawn as the trick she was when you saw her in the club that night. We always said we would never let a bitch come between us."

Right then Gerald had heard enough from Jay. "A bitch didn't come between us! You came between us. You created the dog in me, you created it, and then you hated the dog when the dog took your girl. You came between us when you let Nicole crazy ass in my room that night. You came between us when you forgot the rules to the game."

Jay was stunned at the reaction he was getting. Gerald continued, "You do remember the rules don't you? If you have a girl and you are serious about her, let it be known. If you are asked about your girl and you don't claim her then its open season. Remember that. Huh, do you?"

Gerald stormed into his room and slammed the door. Jay sat there on the sofa pondering what to do next. He didn't have enough money to make it on his own. His back was against the wall. "I have 10 days to come up with something. How the fuck he gonna treat his boy like this? That nigga done fucked with me for the last time. I'll fix his ass."

The mall was a spectacular building; three floors, a food court and plenty of shops for spending money. Gerald walked in through the west wing of the mall, going through JC Penny. Outside the mall entrance from the department store was the picture studio he was suppose to meet Destiny at. As he walked around the department store, he noticed a woman staring at him from the top floor as she got off the escalator.

"Damn, I hope the bitch don't speak to me," he said to himself, as Nicole waited for him to step off the elevator. As soon as his foot stepped off the escalator, she was right in his face.

"Don't act like you don't know me, Gerald!" She walked up and tried to hug him.

"Back up Nicole, I don't have shit to say to you."

"Oh, so it's like that right? Fuck me then leave me, right?"

Nicole was beginning to make a scene in the mall in front of everybody on the second floor, including Destiny, who was getting on the escalator from the floor below.

"Lower your fucking voice!" Gerald snarled, as he looked around to see if anyone was paying them any attention.

"I gave you the best I had and you hurt me like this. Why Gerald, why?" Nicole started crying and really laying it on thick for anyone that was listening or watching. She acted as if she was auditioning for the lead role in The Color Purple. Some real, you told Harpo to beat me type shit.

As she went on with her acting, Destiny was on the same floor as the two of them, but standing a few feet behind Gerald, he had no idea she was listening. She started to walk over and see what was going on but then Gerald gave her every reason to stay where she was.

"This is the reason why I never called your crazy ass after that night. You the kinda bitch that no nigga would get serious about. Nobody will ever take your silly ass home to meet their mama. Don't no nigga want you running around acting a damn fool with his last name. You're the kind of bitch that a nigga just fuck to have something to do."

"Fuck you nigga, you ain't shit! But I bet I get your ass when I file for child support."

Gerald mouth fell open. Everybody within earshot sounded like they all gasped at the same time. A few guys walked by and heard what Nicole had said were talking to each other, "That's fucked up; she put all that man business in the street."

"I'd knock that bitch out if that was me."

Everybody was stunned, none more than Destiny, "Gerald, what the fuck is she talking about?"

Gerald turned around to see Destiny walking towards him. Her pace was fast and the look on her face was rage. Gerald's mouth fell open in shock. Before he could say any-thing she walked past Gerald and got right in Nicole's face.

"Look bitch, I don't care if you having his baby or not, he's my man and you will back the fuck off him."

Nicole was not one for letting someone walk up in her face stood her ground. "I guess you his new bitch, well guess what, I am having his baby and it ain't a damn thang you can do about it. Every dollar that nigga make is coming to me, bitch."

Mall security was walking up as the two women were nose to nose. Gerald grabbed Destiny and pulled her away before they got there. Security walked over to Nicole, "We are going to have to ask you to leave the mall. You are causing a scene and disturbing paying customers." Nicole tried to ignore them as she watched Gerald pull Destiny away from her. Since she didn't move, one of the security guards grabbed Nicole's arm.

"Ma'am?"

"Get the fuck off me, Boy Wonder. Don't fucking touch me. I'm leaving this shity ass mall anyway. All y'all sell up in here is a bunch of stripped polo shirts anyway. I have never been to a mall where everybody sells the same fucking thing. I'm going across town to the classy mall. Y'all can have this ghetto shit hole." As Destiny and Gerald walked away, Nicole gave one last parting shot, "Tell me how my pussy taste next time you kiss that nigga!"

Destiny stopped, looked over at Gerald and asked a question loud enough for everyone to hear. "Why is it fat girls always wear those tight ass baby t-shirts showing every roll on their back, sides and gut? Better yet, I should ask Nicole."Nicole's face was stuck looking dumb as hell as everyone was now looking at her standing there with her tight baby t-shirt on, looking like a muffin top with her belly hanging over the front of her pants. Gerald was surprised that Destiny stood up for him. He knew in his heart that she was the one that he could love for a lifetime. Once out the store, he really didn't know what to say to her.

"Thank you for not trippin' on me about that crazy ass girl."

Destiny snatched around and looked Gerald right in the eyes, "Did you fuck her without a rubber?"

"No."

"Don't stand here and lie to my face Gerald! Did you fuck her without a rubber on?"

I had one on and it didn't break. I think she just said all that to make a scene."

"Well y'all need to get some kinda test done, cause I'm not gonna have that bitch in my face for the rest of my life. Besides, you need all the money you can get to take care of our baby."

Gerald was at a loss for words, he just stared at her for a second. "What do you mean our baby?"

"Just what I said, I think I'm pregnant." Gerald scooped her up in his arms and kissed her with all the passion he had in him. "Oh, my God baby, how far along are you?"

"Only a month or so, my monthly was late so I took a test and found out. I made a doctor's appointment for next week, if you want to go."

"Hell yeah I'm going. I want to be there for everything."

"You better be I'm trusting you with everything I have, cause I love you."

"I love you too."

Nicole walked out the mall furious. She knew that she was not pregnant, but her anger got the best of her. Just the sight of Gerald was enough to drive her over the edge. She thought to herself, Damn, I hate that I love his stupid ass.

Walking to her car, all sorts of thoughts ran through her head about Gerald. She tried to make herself believe she didn't care for him He ain't shit, sorry ass nigga she said repeatedly as she got into her car. Everything she said against him she could find three things that made her love him even more. The more she realized she loved him, the more the hatred grew for Destiny "I'll kill that bitch she ever get in my face again. How could he go for a bitch like that? She's all fat and nasty. What does she have that I don't beside a few extra hundred pounds?" Her jealousy was starting to get the best of her. "I should follow her ass home and fuck her shit up;" As she got into the car, she looked in the rear view mirror at her reflection "I'm beautiful, I'm a classy ass bitch. I'm gonna get my man and I don't care what that bitch says. If I can't have his ass, she sure as hell can't."

The rest of the day Gerald and Destiny were on cloud nine. They held hands as they walked through another clothing store and laughed at each other jokes. Gerald had finally become the Gerald of old; the Gerald that would do anything for the woman in his life. He felt good knowing that he had the woman of his dreams next to him. He had forgotten all about the little episodes with Dawn and Nicole. All he had to do was get Jay out of the apartment and his life would be perfect.

Back at the apartment, Jay was trying to figure out his next move. He had no idea that Gerald and Destiny were still together. "I'm getting my girl back since I know she didn't fall for any of his bullshit this morning. He wants me out by the end of the month, he better hope his ass is still around at the end of the month. If that nigga think I'm just gonna leave like a punk, he's got another thing coming."

A week after the fiasco in the mall with Nicole, Destiny was still flying high. She was so happy that things between her and Gerald were going great. He was turning into everything she ever wanted him to be.

****************************************

Monday morning 9:00A.M.

Destiny stood in her bathroom mirror making sure everything was in place, as she got ready for work.

"Damn I love that nigga," she said, looking in the mirror with a huge smile on her face. She grabbed her black COACH purse, picked up her keys, and headed to the door. Nicole was the furthest thing from her mind as she walked out of her front door.

After turning around to lock her door, she heard a familiar voice that sent a chill down her spine. "How my pussy taste bitch?" Destiny turned quickly, startled by Nicole's rough and scratchy sounding voice. The second her head turned in the direction of the voice, Destiny was met with a blinding punch to the side of the head. All she saw was a flash of light and different color spots as she fell to the ground. She quickly tried to gather herself. Her purse fell out of her hand, and everything in it spilled onto the pavement.

Nicole was like a shark with blood in the water. She didn't give Destiny a chance to get up before she hit her again, square in the face. Destiny again tried to get up but was met with another solid punch to the side of her head. She fell to the ground again. This time as she hit the ground, Nicole's voice was ringing in her ears. "I told you I was gonna fuck you up!" Nicole reached down and pressed Destiny's head down on the ground. "Gerald's my man bitch, remember that!"

Destiny yelling from the top of her lungs, "Get off me bitch, get up!"

Nicole sat on top of Destiny's chest and continued, "Yeah, you thought that shit in the mall was cute." She took her nails and raked them across Destiny's face drawing blood from the corner of her left eye. "Let's see if he still want your stank ass after I'm done." Nicole repeatedly scratched and punched Destiny in the face. Blood was starting to gush from Destiny's nose and mouth. Destiny tried to cover her head as much as possible, but the punches were coming to fast. Destiny kicked and screamed for someone to help but the help never came. She lived in a building where everybody was already at work by 9:00 a.m. The entire beating lasted for only a few minutes, but it seemed like forever as the punches rained down repeatedly. When Nicole was finally done, she stood over Destiny, reached down and grabbed Destiny's face. Looking directly in her eyes and speaking in a soft whispered tone, "I'm not gonna tell you again, stay the fuck away from my man bitch. Next time, I'll kill your ass." Nicole got up and turned to walk away. Destiny lying on the ground grabbed her stomach and curled up in a ball and started praying her baby was ok. What was supposed to be a silent prayer was anything but. Nicole heard the cries to the lord and stopped dead in her tracks.

"What did you say bitch? You pregnant?"

Destiny knew better than to repeat the words that were meant for God, but overheard by satin herself. Nicole walked back over to Destiny and kicked her directly in the stomach. Destiny saw the kick coming and turned her body so the kick actually hit her in the back. Again Destiny curled up protecting her unborn child.

Nicole walked away as if nothing had happened. Destiny laid on the ground crying until she was sure Nicole had left. She braced herself against the door to her apartment. She struggled to get the key in the lock. As she unlocked the door, she almost fell in her front room when the door swung open. Struggling to walk, she made her way to the bathroom to clean her face and to see what damage Nicole inflicted. Her eyes were nearly swollen shut and the blood was still running from her nose. Scratches were all over her face, some deeper than others, and the blouse she wore was totally covered with her own blood. Destiny broke down in the bathroom crying trying to figure out what Nicole was hoping to gain by doing her this way. She walked over to the phone and called Gerald.

"Hello?" his voice sounded scratchy because he was still in bed after a long shift at work.

"Baby, she was over here," she said, crying hysterically

"Who was over there?"

"Nicole."

"How the fuck did she find out where you lived?"

"I don't know, but she was here and she jumped on me."

"Are you aiight?" Gerald said, now sitting straight up on the bed.

"She scratched my face up pretty bad and she kicked me in the stomach."

"Have you called the police?" he asked, pacing around like a caged animal.

"I'm not calling them; I'm going to get that bitch!"

"Baby, stay calm. I'm on my way over. Don't do anything silly. I'll be there in a minute."

Gerald jumped out of bed and looked for something to put on. "That bitch done lost her damn mind!" he said aloud, as he dressed. "Damn, I hate silly bitches."

As Gerald walked towards the door of the apartment, he noticed Jay was asleep on the sofa. He just stood and stared at him for a second. He knew Jay had something to do with this situation. He didn't have any evidence but it was just a feeling he got in his bones. "Jay!" he barked.

Jay was not sleeping that hard and woke up as soon as he heard his name. "What man?"

"Did you give Nicole directions to Destiny's house?" He sounded almost like Jay's father rather than his roommate.

"No, why?"

"She was over there this morning and jumped on Destiny."

Chuckling a little, "That's fucked up, but I didn't tell her."

"Then how did she know?"

"How the hell am I supposed to know? Maybe she followed her."

"Maybe, but I doubt it." Gerald walked out the door, knowing in his guts that Jay was guilty.

Jay sat there for a second then reached for the telephone.

"Hello?"

"Nicole, I see you found the apartment this morning without any problems," he said laughing out loud, now that Gerald was out of the apartment.

"Yeah I found it, and I beat that bitch's ass. It's been a long time since I kicked somebody's ass like that."

They both laughed as if they had heard the world's funniest joke. At one point Nicole started choking she was laughing so hard, as she talked about the sounds Destiny made after each punch.

"I hope you didn't fuck her up to bad."

"Shit, I tried to rip that hoe's face off."

"I feel ya, and I'm gonna get ya boy before it's all said and done."

"I catch them together again, I'm going to both their asses with some permanent shit," she said, sounding as serious as she possibly could.

"Like I said, I got ya boy."

"He is still my boo, so leave something for a sistah."

"We'll see."

"Oh by the way...", before she could finish her sentence Jay hung up the phone, thinking to himself, fuck leaving something. I'm taking that nigga's ass out.

Over at Destiny's apartment, Gerald was soaking a bath cloth to wipe Destiny scratches on her face. "I still think you need to call the police."

Destiny was not listening to him. She was deep in thought trying to figure out a way to get her hands on Nicole. Gerald walked up to her and handed her the towel. "You know I think Jay gave her directions over here."

"I don't think he would do that to me. I know he's hurt and all but to have somebody come over here and fight me; that's a little extreme, even for him."

Although Jay and Destiny were no longer together she still felt like he would not do anything to hurt her.

"That nigga is just as silly as she is and I wouldn't put shit past him," Gerald said, as he wiped her face with the cloth.

"Do you think he would do anything to you?"

Gerald all of a sudden got quiet. He never gave it a second thought that Jay would do anything to him. He knew that Jay was a little off, but not that off. "Nah, his only beef with me right now is you and I don't think he'll stoop that low over a female."

Destiny did not like the fact that Gerald was so calm about living with Jay. "When is your lease up?"

"March, why?"

"I want you to move in here with me"

Gerald's mind drew a blank when looking for an answer. He just stood there looking like he had seen a ghost.

"Are you serious? That's a big step baby."

"I know, but I want you here with me and the baby."

"Do you really want me here, or do you just want me away from Jay?"

"A little of both, to be perfectly honest with you."

Gerald just stood there smiling like it was Christmas morning. "I tell you what I'll do, I'll let Jay sign the new lease and stay at the apartment, and I'll move in here with you."

Destiny jumped into Gerald's arms with happiness. The two would be together without any outsiders coming in messing things up. Her perfect little family would be together forever.

Back at Gerald's apartment, Jay has just got home from walking up the street to the All American Gun Shop. "I'll put these in later." He slid the box of bullets under the sofa. "I need some pussy to get my mind off shit" He picked up the telephone and called the chat line. Within 5 minutes, he had a young woman on the line and ready to come over.

"So, I'll see you in 20 minutes right?" Jay asked in a demanding tone.

"Yeah I'll be there; I know exactly where you live."

Jay hung up the phone and went to take a shower. As he undressed and stepped into the hot water, all he could think about was hurting Gerald. I should kill his ass tonight when he gets back, he thought to himself. "That nigga stole my happiness; my girl, my life, and think I'm gonna stand back and let that shit happen!" He said, as his rage again started to show.

He stood in the shower and let the scorching hot water run all over his body. The steam in the shower was thick because the water was so hot. His entire body was red from the near boiling water. The pain he was feeling is the pain he wanted Gerald to feel. The more painful the water got the madder at Gerald he became.

Ten minutes later, there was a knock at the door. Jay opened the door and a young woman that was in a size 16 dress that needed to be in a size 20 was standing at the door. He watched as her abundantly plump derrière jiggled with every step she took. She was not the typical woman that Jay would normally go for but today was a different situation. He just needed to get his mind off Gerald for a while and anyone would do. Jay was not in the mood for a lot of small talk.

"Take off your dress," he demanded, as the young woman sat down on the sofa.

"Damn, you ain't gonna offer me anything to drink or ask my name, just right to the point, huh?"

"Don't make sense going through all that. You know why you're here."

The young woman did what she was told and let her dress fall to the floor. She stood in front of him in a huge white cotton bra with matching underwear. She unhooked her bra and Jay watched as her large breast fell almost to her waist. She motioned for Jay to stand in front of her.

"I'm a suck the hell out your dick." She took him into her mouth and began to slowly lick on the tip of his penis.

"If you gonna suck the dick, suck the dick! Damn all that lickin shit."Jay was growing irritated with her. She lowered her mouth all the way down over his manhood. "That's it; yeah suck my dick," Jay was beginning to enjoy the technique of the young woman. She would deep throat him really slow, them massage the tip of his penis with her tongue really fast. Her mouth was really wet and she gently tugged on his balls while she performed for him.

"Want me to suck them balls baby?"

"Hell yeah. Do what you do." Jay's mind was still on Gerald and getting him back while the young woman tried her best to get him off. "Put your ass in the air so I can hit it from the back," he bluntly told her. Once again, she did as she was told. Her dimply behind was high in the air waiting for Jay. He placed both hands on her butt as he slid his erection into her. "Damn you wet. You get this wet from suckin dick?"

"Sucking dick gets me wet as hell, I love it." She answered damn near out of breath.

Jay did not waste any time getting into a rhythm. He was slamming into her with ease.

"Fuck this pussy baby!" She yelled as he plowed into her. With every stroke, her butt wiggled uncontrollably.

Fat bitch, Jay thought to himself as he watched the show her butt was putting on.

"Let me ride you boo."

Jays eyes got big as saucers, "Nah, I like it like this." what he really wanted to say was, You done lost your damn mind if you think I'm a let your fat ass get on top of me. The question she asked was the only thing that took Gerald off Jay's mind for a second. He squeezed her butt while he entered her over and over again. The more he thought about Gerald the harder he began to slam into her. Without realizing it, he was pounding away at the young woman.

"Hey nigga, calm down a little. The pussy ain't going anywhere."

"Shut the fuck up Destiny!" he yelled as he pressed down on her back to get better leverage.

"Stop, who the fuck is Destiny?" The young lady asked but Jay was too far gone to realize what he was saying.

"You gonna leave me for that nigga! You think he got dick like this, huh? This my pussy."

The young lady tried to push herself off the sofa but Jay had her pinned down. One of his hands was on her back and the other was on the back of her head holding her down.

"Yeah Destiny, take this dick! As much as I love you, then you hook up with my friend. Hell naw; I'm gonna beat the hair off this pussy." Every hard stroke into her Jay thought was a punch to Gerald.

"Get the fuck off me!" She finally was able to flip off the sofa. Both of them hit the floor and she scrambled for her clothes.

"What the fuck wrong with you bitch? I was about to nutt!"Jay was in a trance like state when she flipped him off of her.

"Fuck you nigga! I told you to stop." She quickly got dressed. She headed for the door with her shoes and bra in her hands. "I should call the police on your stupid ass."

Jay sat on the sofa "Bitch please. I wish you would call the police. I didn't rape you; you came over here and got the hell fucked out of you. Don't blame me because you couldn't handle the dick."

"Fuck you nigga! Ole punk ass nigga," She slammed the door behind her. Jay laughed out loud after she was gone.

"I needed that; she was just what I needed to get my head on straight."With that, Jay sat out to come up with the perfect plan to get even with Gerald.

It was two days before the end of the month. Gerald had decided that since Nicole had paid Destiny a visit a few days ago that it would be best not to wait till his lease was up in a month, but, to move in immediately. Gerald woke up early to start moving his things. With all the commotion in Gerald's room, Jay woke up wondering what was going on.

"Dawg what are you doing so early in the morning?" Jay was still trying to wake up when Gerald walked into the front room and sat down.

"Jay, we need to talk."

"'Bout what?"

"I'm moving out today."

"Movin out?"

"Yeah I have another place to stay, so I'm gone take all my important shit, and you can have everything else."

When Gerald first moved to Greensboro, he purchased the sofa and chair set from the local Goodwill. It was not in the best of conditions but it was clean and was within his price range and anything is better than sitting and sleeping on the floor. He paid $100.00 for the entire set and it had severed its purpose. Jay sat up still trying to fully wake up by rubbing his eyes and wiping the overnight slob from the side of his face.

"Where you moving to?" Jay asked, sounding as sad as he could.

"An apartment on the other side of town."

Jay's eyes squinted a little trying to think of a place on the other side of town Gerald would want to stay. All of a sudden Jay's face looked as if he had just figured out the million dollar question.

"You moving in with Destiny?"

"Yeah, Since Nicole pulled that shit the other day, I'll just feel better being there with her."

"That was fucked up what she did," Jay said, knowing that he was the cause it.

"Yeah it was, but it will never happen again. I'll make sure of that."

Jay was still concerned about the upcoming rent for the next month. "So am I gonna have to pay the entire rent for the rest of the lease?"

"Well, that's where it's gets a little funny."Jay sat there listening to every word that fell from Gerald's mouth. "I went down to talk to the leasing agent the other day and she cut me a deal. She said I could break the lease a month early but I had to be out of the apartment by Sunday."

Jays was confused, "What Sunday?"

"Tomorrow."

Anger flowed through every vein in Jay's body. Gerald had gotten back at him for telling Nicole where Destiny lived. Gerald had a very jovial look on his face. He knew he had just cut Jay to the core by giving him one day to find a place to live.

"What the hell do you mean tomorrow?"

"Tomorrow as in 24 hours from now, day after today, the day before Monday. However you want to look at it; tomorrow."

Jay jumped to his feet, which made Gerald stand up. He was thinking that Jay was gonna rush towards him to fight.

"What the fuck am I suppose to do, I don't have any place to go, I thought I had till the end of March."

Gerald shrugged his shoulders nonchalantly.

"I don't know what to tell you on that one. But they are coming to clean the apartment Monday morning. They expect me to be out of here and since you never went and got put on the lease, that means if I'm gone, you're gone." Gerald didn't want to smile but it felt great putting the screws to Jay. There was no friendship there and it didn't make sense to try to make things right for Jay when Jay was the reason things were falling the way they were.

"You ain't shit Gerald! You knew what you were doing when you went down there to break the lease. You knew I didn't have a place to go yet."

"Here we go again, saying I ain't shit. I told you to get your name on the fucking lease. Did you ever do it? ...No. I told you, you had to find another place to live, did you go look? No. So now your ass is on the street after tomorrow. Is that my fault? No."

Gerald turned away and walked into his room. Jay sat on the sofa mad as ever. He didn't know what to think. Rage consumed him. He reached under the sofa and pulled out the chrome Thunder380 pistol that he purchased on his walk after he found out that Gerald and Destiny were seeing each other. He loaded the clip with the bullets he bought a few days ago. His hands shook as he loaded the bullets in one by one. Sweat was starting to bead up on his forehead. "Fuck this shit, I'm gonna kill his ass!"

Jay stood up and took a deep breath. In his heart he knew what he was about to do was wrong, but his mind was telling him to go in Gerald's room and shoot him dead. Jays mind was running a mile a minute as he walked towards the room. He thought about all the fun times they had mistreating women, having all the sex two men could ever want. He thought about the day they met at college, all the Thanksgivings and other special holidays they spent at one another houses. With a blink of his eyes, all of the good memories were gone and the vision of Gerald's dead body was plastered in Jays head.

As Jay walked slowly to the door hoping to surprise Gerald, the telephone rang. Gerald answered the phone "Hello.......He's right here, hold on a second....Jay get the phone, it's your mama."

Jay stood inches away from Gerald's door with his hands shaking and sweat running down his face. He turned and walked back to the sofa quickly. He slid the gun back under the sofa. His moment of rage was over. There was no way he could shoot Gerald with his mother listening on the phone.

"Aiight, I got it"

While Jay was on the phone with his mother, Gerald was busy packing his car with all his belongings. He left the sofa set and a few dishes, but everything else went with him. Jay tried to rush his mother off the phone but she kept him occupied by asked a lot of questions about him and Destiny. She had not talked to him about it since he was home for Christmas. "No Ma, we are not together anymore"

"What happened?"

"I really don't want to talk about it right now."

"Well if you want to talk, mamas always here."

"O.K., no problem"

"So, how's Gerald doing? I talked to his mother the other day and she said that he has a baby on the way."

Jay stomach balled up in a tight knot. His head began to pound. He felt like he was about to throw up everything he had ever eaten. "Does he? He didn't mention that to me."

"Yeah, she told me that he was very excited about being a father. What kinda roommates are y'all? You didn't know your best friend was having a baby?"

"Ma I gotta go, something just came up".

Jay slammed the phone down on the receiver. His eyes were glossy, he felt like he was about to cry. His entire insides were turning. The thought of Gerald having a family with Destiny was way too much for Jay to handle. Jay sat on the sofa in complete shock. He couldn't hear anything but the ticking clocks on the wall across from him. Everything sounded muffled as he tried to pull it all together. He looked into Gerald face and saw that he was saying something to him but he couldn't hear him. Jay just sat there looking into space. Boom, the front door closing behind Gerald snapped him out of it. He jumped up, reached under the sofa grabbed his gun and ran into Gerald's old room. He opened the closet door and nothing was in there. The sheets were off the bed and all of Gerald's cologne and other toiletries were gone off the dresser. He noticed a note that was taped to the dresser mirror. Please deliver this bed room set to 225 Lakeview Dr. Apt B., the note was left for the movers. Jay sat on the edge of the cold bed

"That nigga got her pregnant," he said to himself as tears ran down his face. He placed the gun to his head and was tempted to pull the trigger. He felt he had nothing more to live for. Even if he did win Destiny's heart back he could never love Gerald's child. The gun barrel was pressed hard up against his skull; he closed his eyes and took a deep breath. His heartbeat got faster as he put pressure on the trigger.

"Fuck it, I can't do this." He put the gun down and damned the day Gerald was born. "I swear I'ma kill his ass, Nah I'll do one better than that. I'ma kill his ass in front of Destiny. I want her to feel my pain." Jay stood up and turned around looking at the bed. He pulled out his penis and began to urinate on the mattress. "Lay ya head on that nigga!"

Sunday afternoon Jay started moving his things into Greensboro City Inn. There he could rent a room by the week. The hotel was located right on the outskirt of downtown. It was a place where a lot of people that fell on hard times could rent a room and live till they got on their feet. The only bad part was very few of them ever got on their feet. The place smelled like piss from the time you walked in to the time you walked out. It was the type of place you never sat your drink down in. You never knew what was going to crawl in if you did.

Getting to work was not a problem since Jay worked a few blocks away at a new and trendy restaurant. Jay had his new best friend come over and help him move.

"Thanks for helping me move, Nicole."

"Not a problem, it's fucked up how Gerald did you."

"It's all good. He'll get his, trust me."

Nicole hugged Jay's neck and began walking down the stairs from his room. As she walked away Jay got an idea on how to make Gerald and Destiny's life miserable. Jay leaned over the upstairs rail.

"Did you know Destiny's pregnant?"

Nicole snatched around very fast. With everything going on, it slipped her mind the Destiny was carrying Gerald's unborn child.

"When did you find out?"

"I found out yesterday. She was over the house helping him move all his things when she told me."

Nicole's face turned bright red. You could see the muscles in her jaw move as she became enraged.

"I told that bitch to stay away from him! She just keeps inviting me to beat her ass. Now she wants to run around and tell people that she's pregnant by my man. Oh hell nah."

Jay continued to add fuel to the fire, "Yeah, she was all bragging about how she kicked your ass and she'll do it again if you come around her or her man."

Nicole started pacing around the car. Her fists were clinched as she walked back and forth shaking her head. "That bitch never even hit me back. All she did was ball up like a ball and scream like the bitch she is.

Jay watched and Nicole had a classic melt down right there in the middle of the hotel parking lot.

Screaming in a high pitched, almost ear shattering tone, "That bitch trapped my man. That's just like a ghetto hoe to play games like that!"

Jay watched as Nicole went off the deep end. He knew if Nicole handled her part, his job would be easy. And, from the looks of it Nicole was gonna do a lot more than just handle her part.

*******************************************

Gerald laid on the couch in his new apartment. Destiny's apartment was a lot different from where he had just moved. The apartment was fully furnished. It was evident that this furniture was not from Goodwill, but from the galleries in High Point, North Carolina, furniture capital of the world. The front room was painted sage green and decorated with brass palm trees and pictures of exotic animals on the walls. The 42inch television sat in a mahogany entertainment center. When you turned the TV on, the sound from the Bose surround sound system would engulf you. Destiny had installed just for Gerald. The master bedroom was beautiful. It was painted Beige and the oak queen size bed was a perfect fit in the room. Life was good and the two of them loved living together.

"What did Jay say when you told him you were leaving and he have to be out by today?"

Gerald nonchalantly answered while stuffing cashews in his mouth. "He just kinda looked silly as he always do. Asked me what was he suppose to do. I told him, that was not my problem. He has to find a place because they were coming to clean the apartment Monday."

Destiny walked over and laid on the chaise she had just purchased. "So I guess it's just you and me now, huh?"

"Yep, just you and me. No Jay, no Nicole, ,no Dawn, nobody." Gerald then pulled a small shirt box from under the sofa that was gift wrapped and handed it to Destiny.

"What's this?"

"It's a small token of how much I love you."

She unwrapped the box, throwing the paper on the ground. Inside the box were two round trip tickets to Miami, Florida.

"I want you to go home with me and meet my family."

Destiny was overwhelmed with excitement, "I've never been to Miami before and I would love to meet your family."

"Good, we leave this coming Friday morning"

"So, soon? Damn, I have to go get a few new outfits to show off in the M.I.A."

"I feel you, I'm gonna take you to South Beach, Coco Walk, Bayside, Las Olas, all the hot spots in South Florida. We're gonna have a great time. On top of all that, I really want you to meet my brother Greg. He just got out of prison for something his wife did, but he'll be there and this will be the first time I get to see him in eight years."

Gerald brother Greg had contacted him a few times over the years. Greg and his kids where now living in Orlando, Florida with his girlfriend Lisa. They were all going to meet up at their mother's house for a small family reunion. Gerald didn't see the need to go into great detail about why his brother went to jail, with Destiny.

"Will you're brother wife be there as well?"

"I doubt it seriously. She's locked up as well. Actually, she's locked up for another 15 years."

"Damn what did she do?"

"She had a man killed. That's all I know."

Gerald quickly changed the topic. He didn't want to get into the fact that his brother was the man that actually tossed a man over the side of a cruise ship. He never told another living soul where his brother was. Not even Jay knew where his brother had gone. Whenever Greg came up, Gerald would just change the topic and act like he didn't hear what was being said.

"When you go shopping, don't buy too much at one place. I want to take you to all the different malls down there; Adventura Mall, Mall of Americas, Sawgrass Mills and those are just the ones on my side of town."

Destiny's head was spinning with the news of going to Miami. "How long will we be there?"

"A week, we'll be back next Saturday night."

"I guess when I go in to work tomorrow, I better put in for my vacation then, huh?"

"Yeah you betta, cause if not, I'm still going."

Destiny got up to use the rest room. Gerald took this opportunity to call his brother. "Hey man, wuz up?"

"What's goin' on little brother? I cannot wait to see you. It's been 8 years since I last laid eyes on you."

"I know it's been a minute. I'm bringing my new girl home with me."

"That's good man. I hope you picked a good one, cause the one I had wasn't hitting on shit. That's why her ass is still locked up."

Greg never told a soul that the hatred he has for his ex-wife Rena is because she made him suck another man's dick to prove he loved her.

"Well my girl Destiny is not like Rena at all. She's good people and I think she's the one."

"The one for what?"

"I think I want to spend the rest of my life with her."

"Well I don't know her but if you think she's the one, then follow your heart."

********************************************

Back at the Florida State Prison

The state attorney spoke with a woman that you could tell used to be beautiful. She now looked 30 years older. Her hair was now in dreads and she looked as if nothing anyone said to her would matter.

"Rena Robbins, the state of Florida has decided to suspend the rest of your sentence."Rena never looked up at the skinny white guy that was talking to her. She kept her head down. The years she spent in prison had made her a harder woman. A woman that nothing could bother. "As of tomorrow at 9am, you will have paid your dept to society and will be free to go."

Rena and her attorney turned and walked out of the small room they were just sitting in. "Rena did you hear what he said? You're going to be out of this hell hole tomorrow," Her attorney said with a wide smile on his face.

"Why are they letting me out?" She asked.

"The prison is overcrowded and you've never had a bad day since you've been here. You've never been in a fight and you have shown them that you are not the killer you were made out to be by your husband and his new girlfriend."

Rena stopped walking, "New girlfriend?"

"Yes, Greg's moved on and I hate to be the one to tell you this but, he has the two girls as well."

Rena knew without asking who the girlfriend was. She knew that Greg was going to run to Lisa just as sure as he got out.

"My mother wrote me and told me about the girls about six months ago. I'll get them back in due time."

"Well, go ahead and start packing your things, tonight's the last night you'll spend in this dump."

She finally smiled and walked back to her cell. As she began taking pictures of Greg and Lisa down off her wall she just smiled and suddenly burst out laughing. "Hell I might as well leave a few things here; I'll be back shortly," she said, as she laughed hysterically.

Nicole sat around her apartment trying to figure out a way to get Gerald back in her life. "I'll make him jealous," she said to herself. "I'll get an ex boyfriend to make his ass jealous." In her mind Destiny was only borrowing her man till he came to his senses. Nicole could not live with the fact that a man didn't want her. "That nigga don't know what he's missing, all this fat red ass and big fucking titties. Hell, if I was a dude I'd fuck the hell out of myself."

The more Gerald pushed her away, the more she pursued him. "I'll get somebody to show his ass what he's missing." She walked around her apartment talking to herself like she was in a room full of people. "What simple minded muthafucka can I talk into doing whatever I want?" She sat on the sofa for a second then it hit her. "I could always get Travis to do whatever I wanted him to do. "

Travis was the thug type; the type that didn't really have much going for himself but a hard body and a big dick. Thinking was not his strong suit, but he was the type a lot of girls find very attractive these days. The whole, I need a nigga that's down for me type. Every time you saw him, he was walking around with his pants hanging down, with a White T-shirt on and a scarf tied around his head, looking like a reject Juelz Santana. When you saw him you just knew that nothing intelligent was going to come out of his mouth.

"Wuz up Travis?"

"Who is this?"

"Nicole."

"Hey wuz up girl, long time, no hear from."

"I know, I've been a little busy lately."

"Yeah I feel you, me too."

"I'm a get straight to the point, who you fuckin these days?"

The phone went silent for a few seconds before Travis answered. "Oh shit, wasn't expecting that one."

"Well?"

"Why?"

"I wanna be that female." Nicole knew that Travis still had feelings for her and all she had to do was have sex with him a few times, and she could control his every move.

"Really? We can make that happen, but I have a question for you,"

"What?"

"Who was that nigga you were fighting with in the mall a few weeks back?"

The phone went quiet for a moment, Nicole was trying to think fast of an answer that Travis would believe. "That was this nigga that be stalking me."

"Stalkin you?"

"Yeah, I hollered at him a time or two then that nigga got all crazy, so I had to let him go."

"Damn, he likes that?"

"Yeah, did you hear our conversation that day at the mall?" She wanted to make sure that he didn't hear all the things she said that would blow her plan out of the water before it started.

"Nah, I just saw you and some dude arguing. It was too many people around for me to get close enough to hear what y'all were saying." Nicole breathed a sigh and got her mind back on the task at hand. Travis continued, "So you wanna just fuck, or you wanna be together?"

"Let's take it day by day, I want things to be right between us."

"I'm feelin' that, what about that nigga that be stalkin you?"

"What about him?"

"Do I need to deal with his ass, or what?"

"Yeah, but just scare him a little. He's a weak ass nigga, wanting some pussy he ain't getting."

"I'll deal with him then. When I saw y'all in the mall fussing, I thought to myself that he was not the kind of dude you liked anyway. You like them thug ass niggas like me," He said laughing. "You like the kind of nigga that's gonna beat the hair off the pussy and slap that ass."

"Hold on……….. Let me call you back a little later, that's my girl on the other end."

"Aiight. One"

Travis was the kinda guy that didn't want any man looking or speaking to his woman. He had no problem turning violent if he felt that another guy was disrespecting him by talking to his lady. He was happy that he had Nicole back in his life, but he had no idea she was using him to try and make Gerald jealous.

"Welcome to the Piedmont Triad International Airport," the automated voice said, as Gerald and Destiny walked through the airport doors. Destiny's face was glowing as she and Gerald walked towards their flight.

"I can't believe I'm actually going to Miami!"

"You'll have a good time down there. My family can't wait to meet you."

"I hope your mother likes me."

"She will, but I'm gonna give you a bit of advice. After you meet her she's gonna go into the kitchen and start cooking something. You need to go in there with her and ask if there is anything you can help her do. She'll think the world of you after that, trust me. That will show her that you are trying to be a part of the family. Now if you just sit there and act all unsociable she will never accept you and trust me, on her bad side is not a good place to be."

"I just want to fit in with them."

"You will. I talked to my brother Greg the other day about you."

"Really, what did you tell him about me?"

"I told him that I really love you and that I want to make this work."

"And what did he say?"

"He just told me don't let anything come between us and always remember why you fell in love. He just went through a little situation with his wife that ended horribly."

Gerald couldn't bring himself to tell Destiny the truth about his brother. She didn't need to know that Greg tossed a man to his death because he and his wife wanted the dead man's wife all to themselves. Destiny didn't have to know that his brother's new girlfriend was the woman who snitched out his ex-wife to police which caused her to get put away for murder.

When they reached the airline counter to check in, they were greeted by a young lady with a strange look on her face.

"Tickets and ID please."

They handed her the information and her face frowned a little.

"Is there a problem?" Gerald asked, after noticing the look on her face.

"No, everything is fine." The young lady handed them their tickets and I.D. back. "Have a great trip!"

As Gerald and Destiny walked away, the young lady picked up the telephone. "Nicole?"

"Yeah?"

"Your boyfriend Gerald is going to Miami for a week with some hoe."

"He's going to Miami?"

"Yeah him and some female name Destiny."

"I told that bitch............ nah, nah I'll get that bitch when she get back. What time do they get back here?"

"6:30 p.m. Sunday."

"Aiight, thanks cuz."

Nicole was furious. "How in the hell is he gonna take that tramp to Miami. I'ma fix both they asses when they get back."

She snatched up the phone again.

"Hello?"

"Jay, why the fuck didn't you tell me Gerald was taking Destiny to Miami?"

"Cause I didn't know."

"Well, they'll be down there for a week."

"What time do their plane land back here?"

"6:30 p.m. Sunday."

"Aiight, calm down, it's all good, trust me."

The two hung up the phone. Jay sat in his room staring off into space. "This is perfect; this shit is working out just how I want it to."

Nicole paced around her apartment. "Let me call Travis back and tell him, he needs to take me to the airport next week, it's time to put an end to this shit."

Greg and Lisa in their new life together, was a perfect fit. "Damn I should have married you instead on Rena in the first place." Greg said as he walked up behind Lisa and grabbed a handful of her plump round ass as she put her make-up on to go meet Gerald and Destiny at the airport.

"That's right, but it took you having to do a little time away from me to realize that you needed to have this pussy in your life on a regular basis." They both laughed at Rena's expense.

"Yeah, a little time hell. Seven Years is a long time to be locked up with a bunch of hard dicks looking to go in any hole they could find. Shit, I went weeks at a time without cleaning my ass to make sure I stunk to high heaven to make sure none of them hard ass faggots tried to make me their bitch. I wouldn't even wipe my ass after I took a shit to make sure they could smell me before they saw me."

"OK, a little too much information baby."

Greg laughed and continued to get dressed. After a few minutes Lisa started a conversation that Greg didn't see coming. "So do you ever think about her?"

"Think about who?"

"Lisa stood there for a second, "Rena."

Greg stopped buttoning his shirt and looked over at Lisa in the mirror. "Why did you ask me that? Do you think about her?"

"Yes I do. Every time I look at her kids running around my house."

"Are you saying you want to have a kid with me to call our own?"

"Well, I've been thinking about it."

"Well," he said mocking her, "Get that shit out your head. I do not want any more kids. I have two and I'm done. Besides, you are the only mother these kids know anymore. I refuse to take them to see Rena and if they are anything like the rest of my family, Rena is out of site out of mind."

***********************************

As Rena walked out of the Florida Judicial system forever or at least for the time being, the first person she wanted to see was her mother. The sun hit her face for the first time in seven years as a free woman. She stood in the walkway for just a second and enjoyed what most take for granted; sunshine and the smell of freedom. For years, she had to sit behind those stank ass walls and hear women raping young girls that thought they were grown, until a big butch walked up and made them lick her pissy smelling pussy. The site of her mother sitting outside in her car was the only thing she wanted to see. As she rounded the corner to the outside world, she saw her mother sitting in her Denali listening to her gospel music.

"Baby, it's so good to see you without that think glass between us."

"Yeah mama, I'm happy to see you as well. "

"What's the first thing you want to do?"

Rena sat there for a second, then answered, "Go get in a tub!"

After what seemed like hours in the tub, Rena finally emerged and went into the kitchen where her mother had cooked a meal fit for a king. She had collard greens, corn bread, pinto beans, smothered chicken and white rice. Rena sat to the table and started to eat like she was the hungriest child in Africa. About midway through the meal, Rena asked, "So ma, do you stay in touch with Greg's mother and her friend Brenda?"

"Well Greg's mother and I have not talked since the trial but Brenda and I are still ok, why?"

"Just asking, how's her son Jay doing?"

"He's fine, he moved to North Carolina with Gerald."

"Little Gerald moved out of the nest huh?"

"Girl, he aint little no more. That boy got more women then...."

Her mother didn't finish that sentence, but Rena finished it for her, "His brother."

Her mother just looked away trying desperately to come up with something other than Greg to talk about.

"It's cool ma. I'm past Greg, and I've never had a problem with Gerald or his friend Jay."

The next day Rena and her mother were in Publix Grocery Store and just happen to run into a familiar face. "Rena, is that you?" The voice asked, Rena turned to look to see who was calling her and the biggest smile ran across her face.

"Brenda, how's it going? Long time no see."

"Girl, I know. It's a shame what happened to you and Greg but it's good to see you out and about."

"Yes, it's good to be out."

"Wait till I tell Greg's mom I saw you today."

Rena's eyes widened "Please don't do that. They don't know I'm out and I want to stop by and surprise them. Actually that's why we are shopping today; we are planning a big get together and wanted to surprise them with it. Kinda my way of thanking them for all they've done for me."

It was easy to pull off that lie because one thing about the Robbins family, they were not gonna tell all of their business, so it was possible that everyone knew about her going to jail, but they probably told everyone that Greg had a high paying job over in Australia somewhere as to why he's been missing in action.

"How is Jay doing?"

"Oh he's fine. He's up there in North Carolina with Gerald. Those two are like brothers, the way they are always together and looking out for one another."

"Do you have his number? I would love to catch up with him and see if he'd be willing to catch a flight down here for the get together."

"Sure, I'm certain he won't mind me giving you his number. Y'all were practically family. I think he spent more time at your house than he did mine, before y'all left and went to South Carolina."

Later that night Rena picked up her mother cell phone.

"Hello?"

"Hello Jay, how are you doing?"

"Who's this?" he said, sounding agitated

"Rena."

The phone went silent for a second. Then Jay burst out into laughter, "Wuz up girl? It's been a minute. Last I heard, you got locked up on a murder charge."

"Yeah something like that, but I heard you living with Gerald these days."

"Naw, he moved in with my girlfriend and got her pregnant."

"What the hell?" Rena was lost for words. She was not expecting that.

"Yeah that nigga ain't shit. So when you see his ass down there let him know I have a surprise for him when he gets back."

Rena took this as one of those moments when things just fall in your lap. "Now don't go and end up where I just left. It's not worth it."

"I'll be the judge of that, but why did you call me?"

"I was calling to see if you had heard anything or have talked to Greg these days."

"Naw, I have not talked to him but I do remember Gerald saying something about he and his new girlfriends was living in Orlando. But Gerald is in Miami now, so it's a safe bet that his brother is somewhere close. Those two are still really tight from what I understand."

Rena smiled and damn near jumped out of her skin. "So Greg might be in Miami?"

"Yeah."

"Do their mother still live in the same house?"

"Hell yeah, she ain't going anywhere."

"That's what I was hoping you'd say."

"Welcome to beautiful Miami, Florida!" Gerald said, as he and Destiny walked through the airport looking for their luggage. People were everywhere speaking 20 different languages. Destiny walked really close to Gerald hoping not to get separated. People bumped into to her without saying excuse me. This was foreign to Destiny in North Carolina if people bump into you they say sorry or excuse me. Miami was a different story the people will knock you over and keep going like they never saw you. Gerald weaved in and out of the crowd of people holding Destiny's hand.

"Are the people always this rude!" she yelled, as Gerald walked into an elderly Hispanic woman and didn't stop to say anything.

"Just don't let go of my hand. I'll explain it to you in the car," he said, laughing as he brushed against another person barely acknowledging them at all.

Once they found their luggage and got the rent-a- car Destiny felt a little better. "Now explain to me why everybody, including you, are so rude down here"

"That's the way it is here. Miami is a dog eat dog type city. Nobody has time for I'm sorry or excuse me."

Destiny just shook her head and sat back as Gerald drove up the Palmetto Expressway to his mother's house. From the window of the car she could see the Palm trees and the blue sky Miami is known for.

"How far does your mother stay from here?

"About 20 minutes or so."

"I'm going to roll down the window, I want to feel that Florida heat you're always talking about."

Gerald told her that the heat in Miami was different from the heat in Greensboro. The heat in Carolina is really dry; feels like the sun is sitting on your neck. The heat in Miami is wet. A lot of humidity, as soon as you step outside, you're pouring sweat. It's a sticky kinda hot.

It seemed like everybody was driving 100mph. Cars weaved and darted in and out of traffic like they were at The Daytona 500. Finally they exited the highway onto 17th Avenue.

"Home, sweet Home!" Gerald happily said, as they drove past Scott Lake Park.

As they pulled into the driveway of Gerald's mother house, Destiny tried to remember the rules he had told her before they got on the plane. She stepped out the car and looked at the finely manicured lawn. The beautiful weeping willow tree in the front yard was in full bloom. "Baby why are all the trees in everybody's yard so big and beautiful?" Destiny asked, looking around at all the yards with huge beautiful plants. "It's not normal for these regular house plants to be so big."

Again, Gerald laughed while pulling their luggage out of the back of the rent a car. "The reason the plants are so big is because they are sitting right on top of the septic tanks."

Destiny stood there for a second then it finally hit her. "Eww, that's nasty."

"Nasty hell, that's good fertilizer."

Destiny was raised in a doublewide trailer and this was a far cry from that. The house was 2,800 square feet, white with raspberry trimming. It looked like it would only fit in Miami. The terracotta shingles on the roof just screamed Miami. They walked up to the large double oak doors and rang the bell. They heard a voice from inside. "Ma it's some ugly guy at the door."

"Open the door silly," A teenaged young lady opened the door and jumped into Gerald's arms. "Wuz up baby girl," Gerald said to his oldest niece, Jordyn.

"Nada, what's goin' on with you, Unc?" Jordyn asked, jumping out of Gerald's arms.

Friendly Enemies

"Just here to eat." Gerald walked into the house in front of Destiny. She stood in the foyer and looked at the large oil painting on the wall and the chandelier above her head. Just then she heard and older ladies' voice, "Girl don't stand there when everybody else is in here." Destiny, startled by the woman's voice moved into the family room.

The voice she had heard came from Gerald's mother a very attractive heavy set woman in her early fifties. Destiny walked over as Gerald introduced her to everyone. As she looked around the room she noticed a guy that looked exactly like Gerald maybe a few years older. "Hi I'm Greg, Gerald's brother," he said while extending his hand for a shake.

"Nice to meet you, has anyone ever told you that you look like Gerald?"

"All his life. Just remember I'm older, so he looks like me. Oh, and this is my girlfriend, Lisa."

"Pleasure to meet you Lisa."

"Girl, you messing with these Robbins boys, you don't know what you're in for," Lisa replied, giggling.

Destiny thought to herself, that was a strange comment. She just brushed it off and kept talking to the rest of the family.

Destiny laughed and joked with the entire family for what seemed like hours. They told her about Gerald when he was a child. His sister stated joked about how he used to be afraid of girls and even talked about his ex girlfriends. They were making her feel right at home. Then just like Gerald told her she would, his mother got up and went into the kitchen to start dinner. Gerald looked at Destiny as to give her the go ahead. She walked into the kitchen, "Is there anything I can help you with," Gerald mom turned around with a smile on her face.

"No baby, I'm good I'm not gonna be in here long, I just want to peel these potatoes for dinner."

"Then I'll help peel then."

"OK, pull up a chair."

Destiny looked at Gerald and he had the biggest smile on his face. This trip was turning out perfect already.

As the week went on Gerald and Greg took Lisa and Destiny on a boat ride that sails near all the celebrities' homes around Star Island. They visited the Chef and Apprentice Restaurant, The Cheesecake Factory, The Hard Rock Café and various other restaurants. He took her to the Casinos and they caught a Miami Heat Basketball game at the American Airlines Arena. The trip was not complete till they went to the world famous South Beach. They partied all night on the beach. The streets were full of people that wanted to be seen. Beautiful people dined at outside restaurants as $100,000 cars lined the streets. Every so often they got a glimpse of a celebrity going into or leaving a popular nightclub. They even took a cruise to nowhere; that's when you board a cruise ship and it travel out to the ocean and cruise all over the place while you gamble, drink, and have a great time. Miami was just what Destiny had imagined, beautiful people, great food and a nightlife that was incredible. As they headed back to Gerald's mom house they turned onto I-95 from South Beach. Destiny looked back and saw the bright different color lights and pageantry of Downtown Miami. It was a sight she would never forget.

At 2 a.m. they pulled off the highway and stopped at a gas station for a quick fill up. Greg had been crying all day about wanting to smoke a Black and Mild Cigar. As Greg got out the car, a gray Denali pulled up at the pump opposite them. Destiny leaned over to Lisa, "Is it me, or does everyone down here drive the exact same car?"

"No, why do you say that?"

"Because I've seen that Denali almost every time we've gone somewhere."

"Girl you're tripping. Denali's are very popular so you may have seen a few, but the same one, is highly unlikely."

Lisa pulled out her cell and started texting someone. Destiny saw a slender woman get out of the Denali. She had her purse in her hand and she started walking around to their side of the pump. Destiny watched the woman reach into her purse and she saw the pearl handle of a gun come out. Before she could say a word, Rena was walking up quickly on the passenger side of the car. Lisa looked up and before she could even open her mouth she was met with a blinding flash, and she fell over into the driver's seat; motionless. Destiny covered her head and screamed from the top of her lungs. Her heart was pounding in her chest. All she could do was cover up in an attempt to protect her unborn child. She had no clue who this woman was that had just blown Lisa's brains all over the car, but she knew the killer was not going to leave any witnesses.

Destiny reached for the other door to try to get out. She looked over her shoulder back at the killer and saw Rena aiming the gun directly at her. She screamed again and braced herself for the pain and agony she was about to feel. She had always heard that the streets of Miami were violent, but never in a million years did she expect to be the outcome of a crazed woman on a shooting spree.

Rena began to squeeze the trigger to kill Destiny just for being there and noticed Greg and Gerald running outside of the store and towards the car. She instantly turned the gun on Greg, who realized who the shooter was and stopped dead in his tracks. Gerald dove on the ground and tried to crawl to the car to get Destiny. Rena fired a shot that hit Greg square in the middle of his chest. Gerald covered his head and curled up on the ground. Rena fired again and the second bullet hit Greg right above his heart. He fell to the ground breathless and lifeless. Blood poured from the two holes in his chest.

Gerald still crawling on the ground towards the car heard Rena's voice. "Gerald, I have no intentions on killing you it was your brother and his bitch I had to get rid of. I guess since I have nothing else to lose I might as well tell you how I found y'all. I talked to your boy, Jay a few days ago and he told me that you were coming down and I might as well be able to find your brother with you. Oh and by the way if I were you I'd be careful with Jay, it sounds like he has something for your ass when you get back." Gerald trying not to make a sound listened to how his former friend was responsible for the death of his brother.

Rena continued, "Well I guess I gotta go. I hear the police coming and there is no chance in hell I'm going back to prison. So I guess I'll go ahead and get a jump on kicking your brother's ass in the afterlife." Another gunshot rang out and Gerald saw Rena's body fall to the ground on the other side of the car; blood pouring from the side of her head. He finally reached the car door and saw Destiny lying across the back seat.

"Baby, Please be ok, baby!"

Destiny looked up, tears running down her face with piece of Lisa's brain and scalp in her hair. She was shaking like a leaf blowing in the wind.

"Did you get shot? Are you ok? Baby please talk to me!"

Destiny started screaming hysterically. Gerald wrapped his arms around her in an attempt to calm and comfort her. She squeezed his neck and crying into his shoulder.

After several hours at the police station answering questions about the day's events, Destiny and Gerald went back to their mother's house. She was sitting on the sofa crying as she was flanked by her brothers and sisters; that had all heard the news and came to either be nosey or to comfort her. Either way, she needed to have her family around her at this point. A few minutes after walking into the house Gerald's mom asked to speak to him alone. "Baby I had a dream about you last night."

"I hope it was one that told you to tell me some numbers to play," He said, trying to lighten the somber mood.

"No it was about you."

"What about me?"

"Baby be careful up there. I don't know why, but I feel like something bad is coming your way. And in my dream I saw you lying in a puddle of blood."

Gerald didn't know what to say. He didn't want to seem scared, "Ma I'll be fine, you know me. I'll be aiight."

"I know son, but be careful OK."

"OK Ma, I'll be back in a few days to help with the funeral arrangements."

A few hours later Destiny and Gerald were on their way to the airport. Gerald couldn't help but think about the conversation he and his mother had earlier that morning. "She's always worried 'bout something. I'll be aiight," he thought to himself.

Back in Greensboro, Nicole and Jay were planning on making Gerald's mother's dream come true.

Nicole and Travis were in the airport at 6:15 p.m. "What time does your girl plane land?" Travis asked, unaware that Nicole had him there to see Gerald. He was under the impression that they were picking up an old girlfriend of Nicole's. She knew that if Travis saw Gerald he would automatically think that he was following her again and approach him.

"She should be landing in 15 minutes. She's coming in from Miami."

At the other end of the airport Jay was walking towards the gate Gerald was suppose to come from. He had no idea that Nicole was there with Travis and she was also unaware that Jay was at the airport.

"Flight number 231 has arrived from Miami, Florida," the counter clerk said into the microphone. Jay made sure he didn't get to close and let Gerald or Destiny see him as they exited.

Nicole and Travis sat in the general public section of the airport that was not checked for weapons or anything. With so many people in the airport, Gerald and Destiny walked past Nicole without noticing her, as they went to get their luggage.

"Baby I gotta run to the restroom for a second," Destiny said, kissing Gerald on the cheek.

"OK, I'll go get the car and meet you downstairs to get the luggage."

Travis looked up and recognized Gerald. "Ain't that the dude you were arguing with that day in the mall?"

"Oh shit, he followed me here," Nicole did her best to sound surprised as she watched.

"I've had enough of this!" Travis turned into a man determined to protect his woman. "Ah hell nah, I'ma fuck his shit up. How that nigga gon be following you like that?"

Travis and Nicole followed Gerald towards his car. Jay also spotted Gerald walking out to the parking lot and walked about 200 feet slowly behind him, waiting for the right moment to strike. He pulled the 380 from his waist strap and made sure the safety was off.

As Gerald walked over to his car, Travis walked up, "Hey nigga!"

Gerald turned around to see who was talking. He saw Nicole standing back a few fee,t "Who you talking to dawg?" Gerald stood still as he looked at Nicole staring at him with a crazy smirk on her face. "You, nigga!"

"Who the fuck are you?"

"I'm the nigga who girl you stalking."

Gerald looked as surprised as anyone to hear himself described like that. "What girl I'm stalking? You got the wrong nigga, playa."

"Nah, I got the right nigga. I saw y'all fussing in the mall a little while back."

Right then, it hit Gerald who this guy was talking about. "Nicole, She told you I am stalking her?"

Gerald started to laugh a little as he thought how ridiculous it sounded that he was stalking her, when she is in the airport when he got back in town.

Jay stood back and watched as another one of his plans was blowing up in his face. "Who the fuck is that nigga?" Jay asked himself as he watched Travis and Gerald talking.

Travis walked up close to Gerald, "Oh, I'm funny now?" Travis reached into his jacket pocket and pulled out an old 22 mm hand gun.

Gerald stood back and tried to draw some kind of attention to himself by throwing his hands in the air and talking very loud.

"Get his ass baby!" Nicole screamed out, from the other side of the parking lot.

"Hold up man. Don't shoot me! I swear to you I'm not stalking your girl."

"Shit ain,t so funny no more huh? Bitch ass nigga."

Gerald tried to reach for Travis's hand. A shot rang out and Gerald fell to the ground. Nicole screamed as she watched Gerald fall to the ground holding his stomach. She was in shock. She didn't know what was going on around her. Travis ran off down the parking lot.

"All I wanted you to do was scare him! I just wanted you to scare him!" Nicole screamed, as she cried and ran over to Gerald.

Jay started running over also. When he got to Gerald, he was going in and out of consciousness and losing blood. Nicole ran over and tried to keep Gerald up.

"Wake up baby; I'm sorry, I'm so sorry."

Jay asked Nicole, "Did you see what happened?" as he slipped the gun back in his jacket pocket.

"No, all I heard was a gunshot."

While they were talking Destiny was coming out of the airport doors and saw the two of them and Gerald lying on the ground. She ran over screaming, "What did you do to him? Get away from him!"

Nicole and Jay both backed up a little as Destiny tried desperately to wake Gerald up. "Baby please wake up, somebody call 911!" tears ran down her face as she rubbed his head, hoping that he'd wake up.

She looked up at Jay, "Why did you do this to him?" she screamed, with tears pouring down her face.

"I didn't do anything to him. I swear I didn't."

"Fuck you Jay! You and this silly bitch shot him!"

Nicole spoke up. "Destiny I know you hate me but you have to believe me when I tell you we didn't do this."

"Fuck you!"

The airport police arrived on the scene within seconds, "What happened Miss?"

"They shot my man!"

"Who?"

"Those two right there," Destiny said, pointing to Jay and Nicole.

The police grabbed Jay and Nicole. "Man I didn't shot that dude," Jay yelled, as the police threw him on the ground, face first.

"He's shot and what's this? A gun in your pocket. I'd say you shot him."

A female officer searched Nicole and found nothing. An ambulance drove up and tried to revive Gerald. They were able to get a pulse but he was still not out of the dark. Still unconscious, they put him on a gurney and loaded him into the ambulance. Destiny went along with them.

The police put Jay in one police car and put Nicole in another. Jay was screaming his innocence to the top of his lungs and Nicole didn't speak a word. She was still in shock from the entire incident.

An hour after the shooting, Jay and Nicole sat in separate interrogation rooms and the police station. Jay sat behind a table with his head in his hands looking like a rocking back and forth. Nicole sat in the other room looking as calm as the first lady of the church on pastor appreciation day. She had sat there for about 30 minutes, when a heavy set tall white guy walked into the room and sat across from her.

"Nicole, my name is Detective Gore and there is no sense in beating around the bush. Tell me what happened tonight, so we can all go home and get a good night's rest."

Nicole crossed her legs and sat back in the chair and looked the detective directly in the eyes. "I was at the airport to pick up my cousin after her shift. I saw Gerald walking out of the airport and went over to say hello."

The detective cut her off, "How did you know Gerald? Did the two of you have a relationship?"

"Not really a relationship. We kicked it every now and then but nothing serious."

"So basically y'all were just bed buddies is what you're telling me?"

"Yeah something like that," Nicole responded, half laughing.

"So, why did the young lady at the scene say that you and Jay shot him?"

Nicole leaned a little on the table her entire demeanor changed. Her words were now short and the calm exterior was now rugged and harsh. "That bitch, Destiny is crazy as hell. She has been stalking him and harassing anybody that she saw him talking to. She's walked up on me a few times and I just walked away. But, I told her she had one more time to walk up on me and I was going to have to put her in her place."

"So Destiny is the stalker in all of this?"

"Yes."

"Would you consider her dangerous or a threat?"

"Dangerous yes, a threat no."

The detective changed topics, "So tell me about your boy, Jay."

"He's crazy as hell too."

"Damn, everybody you know crazy except you, huh?"

"It's not like that, but I do know that he wanted Destiny for himself. As a matter of fact he dated Destiny before Gerald did."

The detective sat straight up in his chair. All of a sudden he was paying every word that fell out of her mouth close attention. Nicole continued, "Jay hated Gerald for stealing her away from him. He told me on several occasions that he wanted Gerald dead. He even scratched up Gerald's car and busted his windows out. But after he found out Destiny was pregnant by Gerald, he really went off the deep end."

"Do you think he would have went through with actually killing him?"

"Hell yeah! He would do it in a heartbeat."

At that time another detective walked into the room and whispered something in the ear of Detective Gore. They looked at each other and then the later detective walked out. Nicole sat there looking half guilty but trying like hell not to tip her hand. Detective Gore folded his hands together and looked Nicole straight in her face.

"Who was the guy you were sitting with at the airport?"

**********************************

Over in the other interrogation room Jay sat looking guilty as hell. As soon as his detective walked into the room, Jay started, "Man I didn't shoot that dude. I was at the airport because I like to watch the planes land and take off. It's how I clear my head when I'm bothered."

"Damn man, I didn't say you shot anybody but since you like talking, tell me why you were there with a gun in your pocket." Jay rubbed his head looking around the room desperately trying to find the answer to that question written on a wall.

"I had the gun because these dudes have been bothering me and I felt like I needed to protect myself."

"What dudes?"

"I don't know, these dude that live over by us." The detective stopped Jay before he continued to sound dumb and silly at the same time.

"Look man I know that's bullshit and so do you. Now tell me the truth why were you there with a gun?"

Jay sat in the chair with his head tilted as far back as it could go. Looking up at the ceiling he started, "I wanted to scare him."

"You wanted to scare who?" The detective asked, now fully attentive.

"Gerald, man! That dude just didn't respect me at all. We were supposed to be friends but he did the unthinkable to me."

"What was that?"

"He slept with my girl."

"So you were going to kill him over some pussy?"

"Not just that, he talked to me constantly like I was his child. He made it possible for me to get put out of the apartment when he moved in with her. That cat just wouldn't learn.

"Learn what, from whom?"

"I scratched up his car and he didn't stop. I burst his windshield and he still didn't stop. I tried to do everything I could to show him that dating her was a bad idea, but he still wouldn't stop. So I was going to stop him any way I could."

The second detective just sat there for a second trying to inhale everything that Jay had just put in the air.

"Did you shoot him?" The detective asked bluntly.

Jay with tears running down his face answered, "No I didn't shoot him. I saw this dark skin dude walk up to him.

They exchanged words, and then the shot rang out. Gerald hit the floor and the dude ran off."

"Who was the dude Gerald was talking to?"

"I don't know? I have never seen him before. But I did see Nicole standing a little ways behind him."

"Were they together?"

"I think so."

"Would you consider Nicole your friend?"

"Yes, we're cool."

*****************************************

Over in the other room the Nicole was thinking hard about the question she was asked.

"Who was the guy you were sitting with at the air-port?"

"It was my friend, Travis."

"What is the relationship between the two of you?"

"He's kinda a part-time boyfriend."

"What's a part-time boyfriend?"

"We kick it from time to time."

"Now I'm gonna go ahead and tip you off on something before you sit here and tell me another lie."

Nicole laughed a little and sat back relaxed

"We have a video of the entire incident from the airport security camera. Is there anything you want to tell me before I finish my statement?"

Nicole's face-hardened a little. She didn't know what they saw, but she knew whatever it was she had to get it as far away from her as possible.

"Well Jay and Travis are really close friends. And Travis told me that Jay was going to be at the airport waiting on Gerald to get back. Travis saw me waiting on my cousin and came over to speak. We talked for a few moments."

"What did the two of you talk about?"

"He told me that Jay was going to kill Gerald and he was there to try to warn Gerald before Jay got there."

"So Travis is the good guy in all of this?"

"No not really, Travis walked up to Gerald to warn him and Gerald got all up in his face. Travis being a hot head got upset and the two of them scuffled a little, then a gun went off. I never saw Travis pull the gun and shoot Gerald."

"So Travis had a gun as well?"

Nicole looked around the room for a quick second and then answered, "I never said Travis had a gun."

"Yes you did. You said that you never saw Travis pull the gun and shoot Gerald."

Nicole jumped up angrily, "You're putting words in my mouth. I said he never shot him. Jay dumb ass was the one that showed up with his gun. He was the one that shot him, not Travis!"

"Jay showed up with his gun? So this was a planned ambush?"

"No! See Jay told me that umm. Travis was there with me for a second. I mean..." The cool look of innocence that she once wore like a badge of honor was no longer there. Nicole began to stumble over words and looked like she was caught with her hand in a big bloody cookie jar. "I'm not saying anything else without my lawyer. See y'all trying to pin this shit on me and I didn't do anything. My hands are clean."

The heat fumes were pouring off of Nicole and it was obvious that she was uncomfortable and feeling a little frustrated. Gore spoke to her again, "Sure, your lawyer is coming down the hallway now and he'll probably make us let you go but just so you know we got Travis and he's on his way here now. If your story and his story don't match them I'm going to personally come and get you." He didn't blink one time while talking to Nicole. She stared right back at him, not giving an inch.

159

"I'm certain you had something to do with this. I don't know to what extent, but you had a hand in this. I promise you that I'm going to find out what happened tonight and if I find out you had anything to do with this anything at all I'm going to come at you with both barrels loaded," He said, walking out the door.

After 20 minutes of sitting in the room alone, Nicole was finally released. As she was escorted down the hall by a police officer, Travis was coming in the door.

"Nicole, what did you tell them?"

Nicole looked over at him like she had no clue who he was.

"Nicole! Nicole you hear me. What did you tell them? You better not pin this on me. This was all your idea, Nicole!"

She kept walking as if her name was something else. She never turned around as Travis screamed her name over and over again.

Finally after about an hour, Travis had a moment to tell his side of the story. Detective Gore walked into the room.

"We know you shot him. So is there anything you want to tell us that you think we should know?"

"Yeah, Nicole asked me to shoot that dude. She told me he was stalking her and she wanted me to take care of him for her."

"So Nicole put you up to it?"

"Yeah she's my girlfriend and I had to protect what's mine. So when she came to me with the problem, I dealt with it the way she wanted me to. I mean I didn't mean to shoot him but things got out of control fast and before I knew it, the gun went off and he hit the ground."

"Did Jay have anything to do with it?"

"Who's Jay?"

**********************************

Back in the room with Jay and his Detective, Jay had damn near cooked every brain cell in his head trying to talk his way out of this mess.

"Jay just so you know, Nicole said that you are the one that shot Gerald." Jay's eyes widened to the size of silver dollars. Sweat began to pour down his face.

"I did not shoot him! I' admit I did some foul things. But, I swear I did not shoot him. He was my best friend." Jay's head fell to the table.

The detective cleared his throat and asked another question, "So what roll does Travis play in all of this?"

Jay looked up and the detective, "Who's Travis?"

"From what Nicole said, you and Travis were the best of friends that set out to kill Gerald."

"Nicole's a fucking liar! She is the one that was deeply in love with him. She was the one that wanted him dead because he didn't love her." Jay felt like since Nicole was willing to sell him up the river to save her own ass, he was going to tell everything he knew. She was pissed off at him because he ducked her and left her the hell alone. Once she went into his room while he wasn't there and vandalized his shit. Hell, one time she caused a huge scene in the mall. She was screaming and yelling and she told him she was carrying his baby, which was a lie."

He sang like a bird. Everything that she had ever done was now public knowledge. The detective couldn't write fast enough. Jay went on to tell them about Nicole going over to Destiny's house and beating her up and kicking her in the stomach, knowing that she was pregnant.

*************************************

"Madame, you can go back and see him now." The nurse was looking at me and smiling so I figured everything went well. As I walked into the room, I noticed Gerald lying on the bed, half awake.

"Hey baby, I told you, you were going to be ok."

He looked over at me and smiled. He tried to open his mouth to speak but I wouldn't let him. "Don't try to talk baby, just know that I'm happy as hell you are still here with me." I couldn't hold back crying having my man here with me made me the happiest woman on the planet.

"I have some good news. While they operated on you the police came and told me that they caught the guy that shot you."

I didn't want to leave his side, but it was something that I had to do to make sure our little family would not be touched again. I didn't bother to tell Gerald that Nicole was picked up too, since the police let her go anyway.

I had heard Jay mention what apartments she lived in once during a conversation he and I had. As I sat in her apartment driveway, I couldn't do anything but pray. I had to pray to the lord to forgive me for what I was about to do. As I said Amen, she drove into the parking lot. I sat and watched as she got out of her car and began to walk to her apartment. When she closed her door, I got out of my car and walked over to the door that had just closed moments before. I didn't know what I was going to do or say, but I knew I had to do something. My heart felt like it was going to beat through the skin on my chest. I was horrified and wound up at the same time. It felt like I had a spring on my insides that were wound so tight it was going to explode at any second. I knocked on the door and waited.

"Who is it?" the voice on the other side of the door screamed. I didn't answer. I don't know if it was from being scared out of my mind or the element of surprise I was hoping to achieve, but nothing came out of my mouth when asked that same question a second time. I stood to the side of the doors peephole. I heard the chains on the door fall and the dead bolt locks unlatch. Sweat started racing down my face. My hands shook and when the door finally opened, I just reached back and swung as hard as I could. I felt my hand connect with what felt like flesh and I continued to scratch, claw and pound on Nicole's face.

She fell back into the apartment and I rushed in, slamming the door behind me and commenced to unleash a year's worth of ass beating on her. She tried to cover up as best she could, but this time, the shoe was on the other foot and I was trying my best to end that bitch's life, right there on the floor. I grabbed a hand full of her nappy ass hair and repeatedly smashed her head into the ground. I wanted to give her back all the pain she made Gerald and I feel. I don't know what made me do it but I bit a chunk out of her right cheek as I sat on top of her and continued to beat the shit out of her. She screamed as much as I did when she attacked me, but the only difference was that this time, she was on the receiving end. She finally stopped screaming and just laid there on the ground bleeding from all of the scratches and tears into her skin.

She almost looked lifeless after what had to be a 10 minute ass beating. I was covered in Nicole's blood and could have cared less. I wanted to kill this bitch. I stood over her and asked, "Don't feel good, do it bitch?" I stood there and just looked down at her. For a second, I felt sorry for her but the moment she moved I realized how much I wanted her to die and I can say I did everything in my power to make that happen. I turned to walk out of her apartment when I remembered one more thing. I walked back over to her and rolled her on her side. I took a few steps back, and with a running start, I kicked her directly in her stomach. It felt so damn good. I did it another three times just to make sure if anything was in there it was not gonna come out alive. We don't need anything that she reproduced running around on this planet. I spat directly in her bloody face and walked out of the apartment.

\*\*\*\*\*\*\*\*\*\*\*\*\*\*\*\*\*\*\*\*\*\*\*\*\*\*\*\*\*\*\*\*

As Nicole finally started to stir around from the beating she had taken earlier from Destiny, there was a knock at the door. Nicole picked herself up and stumbled into her bathroom. Both of her eyes were black and her face was scratched all to hell. Her hair was standing straight up on top of her head. With every deep breath she took, the pain from Destiny's kick played again and again. She grabbed a towel off the counter and started to dab at the bruises on her face.

"I'm gonna kill that bitch the first chance I get," she said to herself, as she tried to wipe away the blood from around her nose.

The knock on the door this time was followed by someone yelling, "Police, open up!"

Nicole smiled in the mirror. She turned on the water and tossed water on her face to make it look like she was crying. "This is gonna be easier than I thought. Somebody must have heard what happened and called the cops to come check on me. That bitch is going down for touching me," she said as she walked towards the door. She placed her hand on the knob and began her fake crying. When she opened the door, Detective Gore was standing there with four other officers, weapons drawn.

"I'm so happy to see you detective. Destiny was over here and she attacked me. I want to press charges against her," Nicole said, between sniffs and sobs.

"Well Nicole we are actually here to pick you up and take you to jail."

All of a sudden, the fake crying stopped and Nicole's face was twisted with bruises and confusion. "What did I do? I was attacked by a crazy woman and I'm going to jail?"

"You may have been attacked but you're going to jail for your part in the attempted murder of Gerald Robbins."

"What! I had nothing to do with that! What are you talking about?"

One of the police officers walked behind Nicole and placed her left arm behind her back as he put the handcuffs on her. "You have the right to remain silent," the officer started reading her Miranda rights to her.

Once her Miranda rights were read, Detective Gore gloated, "Nicole, I told you I would be seeing you again if your story didn't match up with Travis. Well Missy, come to find out Travis and Jay don't even know each other. You said they were best friends. Travis also told us that you called him and told him that Gerald was stalking you and you wanted him dealt with. Oh, and by the way your cousin had been fired from her job at the airport for calling and telling you when Mr. Robbins was coming back to town after his trip to Miami. So that little detail in your story didn't help either."

Nicole's tears this time were real and they were pouring out. "You got to trust me when I tell you that I didn't set this up. This was not my plan it was Jay's plan to get back at Gerald for stealing his girl."

"Oh don't worry about Jay, he's not going anywhere for a while either. He admitted to a few things and he was at the airport with a gun and that's a federal offence within itself."

Nicole tried to struggle a little but Detective Gore got in her face. "Do you really want to add resisting arrest to the long list of shit I have on you? I suggest you calm the fuck down and come with no problem."

Nicole calmed down and went without saying another word. Gore turned to her looking her dead in her eyes. "I told you I was going to get to the bottom of this. You're not that bright, you know that. You are one of those people that think they can out think the world but don't have the common sense God gave you. You left to many strings untied Nicole."

It's been a year since our last dealings with Jay and Nicole. Our little family is doing just fine. Destiny and I are closer than ever and our son Greg is doing wonderful. We decided to name the baby after my brother that was killed a little more than a year ago.

I've never been back on the date line since I met Destiny and I've never had a urge to get back on and check it out. I must admit, I think about Jay often. I know I was not the best friend in the world to him and I'm partly to blame for him being locked up in Butner Psychiatric Hospital. Sometimes, I really feel bad about the way things turned out. Then other times, I have to remind myself that Jay knew the rules to the game. He didn't follow the rules and ended up on the short end of the stick. That's not my fault at all.

I've since opened up a small restaurant here in Greensboro. The business is going very well and we are even thinking about opening a second location. Destiny has been by my side every step of the way. I love her tremendously, she's my everything.

With the new restaurant being so successful, I spend almost every free moment I have there. Destiny takes care of the books and I run the kitchen. We are the perfect team. Today seems a little weird I don't know why, but it just seems like something's in the air. I get to restaurant and everything's ok. Destiny has to take the baby to the doctor for a checkup so she's going to come a little later. As usual we are busy as hell for lunch. Our lunch crowd is massive. The restaurant only holds 120 people at a time and we are constantly at full capacity for lunch.

Without Destiny being here, I'm having to run the front and back of the restaurant. It's crazy today. As I'm in the back cooking my quickly becoming famous, Chicken Parmesan one of the waitresses come around the corner.

"Gerald, you have someone out here that wants to see you."

"Who the hell is it in the middle of lunch?" I said, sounding as aggravated as I could.

"I don't know, but she said she wants to speak with you."

"Fine, tell her I'll be out there in a moment." Who the hell would come into a packed restaurant and demand to see the owner? Some folk are just damn rude.

After about 20 minutes I finally emerged from the kitchen. I almost tumbled over at the site of the person that was standing by the register smiling at me. At first I was scared to approach her, not because I'm scared of her, but I'm afraid of what she wanted to say to me.

"Dawn, what's going on?"

"Hey Gerald, How have you been?"

"I've been good. Destiny and I are getting ready to get married and our son Greg is doing well. I'm happy, as I've ever been. As matter of fact I've never been as happy as I am now."

"Wow, I'm glad to hear that."

I will admit she was looking damn good. She had put on a little weight but it was all in the right places. If I was still single I would have been all over her. I noticed a few guys in the restaurant watching our every move. I could tell they wanted to know who she was. I had to pull myself together to finish our conversation. "So, why are you here?"

"Well, I came to claim something I left the last time I was here."

My mind went crazy trying to figure out what the hell she was talking about.

"From the look on your face, I can see that you're a little confused. I left you here and I'm not leaving here without you."

Well I'll be damn! How the hell is she just going to pop in town and take me back with her? This bitch done lost her damn mind.

"You crazy as hell girl, stop tripping. I'm not going anywhere with you. Didn't you just hear what I said? I'm happy with Destiny and she and I are about to get married."

"Yeah I heard you. And I figured you'd need a little persuasion." She reached into her purse and pulled out a 9mm handgun. Everyone in the store stopped what they were doing. I didn't move an inch. All I could think about was being shot again and how much I didn't want that to happen again.

"Look Dawn, I'm sorry I hurt you and I'm even sorrier that you came all this way to do this, but I suggest you leave now. I'm certain someone in here has already called the police."

She looked at me with a smile that could make any man fall in love with her. "Well since the cops are on their way, you only have a little time to make up your mind. Come with me to Miami or come with me to hell. Either way, you and I are going to be together for eternity."

Not a soul in the restaurant moved. It was silent and the only sound you could hear was everyone seeming to be breathing at the same time.

"Dawn, as much as I cared about you, I cannot leave my family for you."

With that, a sharp burning pain ran through my stomach. I fell to the floor shot. I reached for Dawn's leg and another shot hit me in the back. The room went black. This didn't hurt nearly as much as it did before. The next thing I felt was something heavy land on my back. I opened my eyes barely and saw that Dawn was lying next to me on the floor. I heard yelling and screaming then everything fell silent.

**********************************

It hurt me to my core to have to bury my fiancé. Gerald was a changed man and he cared about me and his child more than anything on the planet. From what witnesses said, Dawn shot him in the stomach and again in the back. She was about to shoot him again when a police officer rushed into the store and she turned the gun towards him and he shot her dead with one shot. My world has been torn to pieces. It's been a few years now and I'm trying to pull it all back together. Never in a million years would I have thought my life would be so interesting. It seems like I'm always surrounded by controversy.

My new man has been there for me. He's the only father Greg knows since Gerald died while he was still a baby. We sit and watch Greg run around the park chasing birds and playing with anything he could find. He looks just like his father. I think that bothers my man a little, but he never said anything about it. He's been through a lot himself. He came into my life when I needed someone to hold me, to talk to me, and let me know that everything was going to be ok. I look over at him and realize that I made a few mistakes in my past, but I'm glad we're together. All of a sudden, I burst out laughing.

"What's so funny?" he asks, as he wraps his arm around me and pulls me close.

"Remember that time you gave me that damn family tree book I had to fill out myself?"

The End

# Secrets, Sins and Shameful Lies

**Written by:**
## DeiIra Smith Collard

The much anticipated sequel to her debut novel:

# Love Lust and A Whole Lotta Distrust

# Prologue

Nicole Neatherly-Edwards

"Jason!" My voice echoed through the hollow halls of my home as I stumbled behind Jason. For so many years he has been all that I know. He's been the air I breathe, and my emotional nourishment. Not to mention he feeds the hunger and desire of my body. I watched with tear filled eyes as he packed bag after bag.

"What Nicole?" He shouted in anger as he turned to face me. His fire filled gaze burned holes into my heart. Was it anger or hatred?

"Don't go!" My eyes pleaded with Jason, my lips moved but no words escaped.

"Cole, it's too late. I've been gone." He yelled.

"You don't mean that." I knew there was no way he could. How could he walk out on everything that we had? "How can you leave your family, Jason, your son?" I now stood before Jason. My hands greedily groped him, pulling him closer and closer to me until our bodies were pressed softly against one another.

"Get off of me Nicole, we're done. This ain't a game, girl. I'm out." I watched as Jason walked towards our front door. Part of me felt relief because my son wasn't here to see his father walk out.

"I know this ain't no game, Jason. Please, I need you. Don't you understand that I breathe you, that I can't function without you? We are one and if you leave you will leave me half empty. No one can fill that void within me like you can." He never stopped or glanced back at me. My heart beat quickened. Moving as fast as my legs could carry me I scurried behind him, desperate to stop him from ripping apart our lives. "Jason!" My heart screamed as I saw him reach for the door knob. With the turn of the knob he was gone. I made it to the door just in time to see him get into a pearl white Jaguar.  It was a car that I had seen several times in the parking lot of our center, SLVDLR.  What the hell was he doing with Khia?  I screamed in anguish as my body fell against the floor.  The contents of my stomach churned, causing a flood of nausea.  This pain was too much.  The ache that my heart felt was overwhelming.  I felt as if the ground had been snatched from beneath me.  I looked around my home.  The wall portrait that hung above the fireplace faced me.  Jason smiled standing next to me, our son in the middle.  My face burned with the heat of my fury.   Sorrow no longer motivated my actions, rage consumed me and I was compelled to react.  Operating strictly on my emotions, my legs carried me swiftly to the kitchen.  My eyes raided the space until I found the biggest knife I owned.  The violent patter of my feet echoed throughout my empty home.  My first target was the picture that told a million lies.  Balancing myself on a chair I grabbed the painting and threw it to the floor.  The knife made deep, deliberate slashes as I defaced the portrait, cutting Jason out.

Before I raced to our closest, I grabbed the small can of gasoline he kept when cutting the yard.  The shoes and clothes he had left were thrown across our bed.  His words were on replay in my head.  He was done.  I would show him done.  I tossed the gasoline on top of his clothing, over the bed we shared, the bed we had just recently made love in, then lit a match.  I watched as flames engulfed the bed.  The fire grew higher and higher, stretching its scorching fingers towards the ceiling.  I grabbed my purse, pictures of my son when he was a baby and walked out the house.  Just like the house, Jason could burn in hell.

Carmell Devereaux

I stood in the back of the church facing the wall length mirror.  I asked all of my bridesmaids to leave the room.  I needed to be alone. I was minutes away from walking down the aisle and becoming Mrs. Alejandro Escalante.

I began to say a silent prayer. Even though I knew he was good for me and good to me, I somehow thought I would be more excited on my wedding day. My stomach did summersaults as I eyed myself in the mirror. I had dreamed of my wedding day since I was a young girl. My pearl colored wedding gown was gorgeous. My body twisted from left to right as I inspected myself in the mirror. There was a beautiful lady that smiled back at me. My hair was a fiery red color with hints of blonde flowing through it. The long layers lay against my bare back. The ringing of my cell phone interrupted my thoughts. I thought I had turned it off. I looked at the clock. My wedding would be starting in fifteen minutes. Against my better judgment I reached for it. It was a private call.

"Hello." I asked holding the phone near my ear careful not to mess up my makeup.

"Don't do it Carmell." The sound of his voice flooded my ears. The racing of my heart along with the fluttering of my stomach almost caused me to drop the phone.

"Why are you calling me?" I asked.

"Because I know you don't love him." He spoke. Louis voice was low, barely above a whisper.

"You don't know shit then. I'm ending this call. I told you a long time ago, don't call me anymore." I watched as my skin became a bright red. I spoke in the phone as if it were was a walkie talkie, if I held it too close I might somehow be infected by Louis's venom.

"I know I have your heart and that's all I need to know. I saw it in your eyes that day. You still love me and you know what,. I love you."

"You didn't love me enough to leave her. Did you? You had sex with me and then you walked right into her arms and married her. That ain't love. You love the fact that I was stupid for you, eager to please you. Louis those days are over.

Go to hell!" I shouted and disconnected the phone. Immediately after I had hit the end key, it began to ring. I didn't bother answering it. I let it ring. Tears started to stream down my face. I knew that in some weird twisted way I did still love Louis. After all the dirty and hurtful things he has done, my heart still called out for him. Could it be that I was insane? How could I love a man whose only intention was to hurt me more than the one man that continuously strives to see me happy? It made no sense. I could hear knocking on the door. My mother father was coming to tell me it's time.

I pulled myself together as best I could and got ready for my special day. Each step I took became heavier and heavier. Today should be the happiest day of my life.

"You ready babygirl?" My father asked as he took me towards the entrance to walk me in.

"Yes Daddy." I responded. I smiled at my father and allowed him to lead me to the door. We walked down the aisle arm in arm. There were so many of my family and friends. Some came all the way from Colorado to see me get married. I saw my grandmother. She was smiling, proud that I would finally get married. I knew she was hoping for great grandchildren soon. Alex smiled as I approached him. He was a man that looked as if he had won the lottery. My father placed my hand into his. I could see him through the sheer veil. He smiled as he lifted it, exposing my face. I knew he loved me, more than I could ever hope to be loved by Louis, but there was something crying out in me. Something telling me I had to give my one true love one more chance.

Like raindrops from a stormy sky, my tears flowed down my face. I couldn't even find the words to say to Alex. I shook my head from side to side; afraid to say the words that were trying to find their way to my lips.

I watched as Alex went from happy, to confused and then hurt. He understood what my mouth wouldn't convey.

He slowly let go of my hand, touched my face, and then he was gone.

### Natina Mayes

I stood at the top of the stairs listening to Louis whisper into the phone. My heart pounded against my chest. Its violent thumping bounced off the walls of my hallway. The sound of movement bombarded my ears as I stood motionless and waited for him to come out of the room. After five years you would think we were passed this. I regret the day I ever brought this girl into our lives.

"What do you mean you still love her?" I spoke in a clear even tone. Every nerve in my body tingled as I awaited his answer. Louis looked at me, surprised; I had obviously caught him off guard.

"What you talking about girl?" He asked me. He stepped in front of me attempting to go downstairs. I wouldn't let him pass.

"You know damn well what I'm talking about. I know you were talking to Carmell. Louis I thought we were done with this." I looked into his eyes. He shifted them downward to the left before answering me.

"We are." He said.

"You lying son of a bitch. I just heard you. I am standing here carrying your child and you have the nerves to call her and plead with her not to get married. Did you forget that you are married to me?" I stared at him and he stared back.

"Natina, you need to get out of my face. I said it's done. We're together and we always will be, now go sit your ass done somewhere, before..."

"Before what? Before you hit me like you used to? Before you assault your pregnant wife cause she caught you whispering to your whore?" I stood angry before my husband.

I could feel my baby fluttering in my stomach, shifting from side to side as I talked.

"Move Natina." Louis shouted as he tried to move pass me. I was done with this conversation. Too many times Carmell Devereaux had crept back into our live life causing devastation and turmoil and I wasn't having it this time. It's done.

I locked eyes with Louis and wouldn't let him pass. "Move girl." This time he pushed past me with more force. In an attempt to stop him I lost my balance. I struggled to catch myself. Louis hurried behind me attempting to stop me from my spiraled tumble downward. Gravity worked against me. I rolled myself into a ball trying somehow to shield my unborn baby from harm. My body thumped against the hard wood floor, rolling twice before coming to a complete stop. The ache from the fall rushed through my entire body.

My hands massaged my stomach, silently begging my baby to move. A flood of relief washed over me as I felt the baby began to move. It was a faint flutter, then violent spasms.

"Baby, are you okay." I heard Louis. Everything seemed to move in slow motion at this point. I could feel his hand reach for me and try to help me up.

"Agggghhh." I screamed in agony as I stood to my feet briefly before falling to the floor again. Another wave of pain hit me. The pain was coming minute after minute. I took long deep breaths, trying to manage the pain. "Call 9-1-1 baby, I think I'm in labor." I watched as Louis hurried to find the phone.

A tiny pool of blood had begun to form around me as the pain continued. Louis's panicked voice gave the 911 operator our address.

"Baby, I'm so sorry, they're coming, they're coming and you and our baby are going to be okay." I looked up at Louis and prayed he was right. I repeated those words all the way to the hospital.

"God, please ..." I whispered as they rushed me through the ER.

Kendra Dubois

The ringing doorbell chimed throughout our home to signal a visitor. Cory and I sat in the family room watching First Sunday. We need a little laughter in our lives at this time. Weeks had passed and I swore that this time would be different. This time I would really be done. I hit pause on the remote and went to answer the door. My entire body went numb as I looked out the glass in the center of the door. I stood at the door paralyzed, scared to open the door but terrified not to.

"Who is it?" I could hear Cory moving behind me and before long I could feel him standing behind me. We both stared at the door, but he moved first. His fingers moved swiftly as he unlocked and opened the door.

"What the hell are you doing at my home? Didn't I make it clear that this would end?" There was a fire burning in his eyes.

"It doesn't matter what you say, Kendra hasn't said it." Her words were meant for him, but her eyes never left mine. I found myself short of breath as I watched her go back and forth with my husband. I couldn't move, I couldn't speak, I could only stand and watch. I was no more than a voyeur and I was watching my life.

"Tell her Kendra." My eyes shifted to Cory as he spoke. There was so much hurt there in his eyes, so much pain that I knew I had caused. I then turned my attention to Gia. She pleaded with me, looking into my eyes silently saying that she loved me. I didn't speak; not because I didn't want to, but because I couldn't. My voice had vanished.

Gia moved first, stepping into our home, stepping towards me. She reached for me and I saw Cory grab her hand. I could see her wince from the pain.

"Get the hell out of my house." He said again, firmly.

"Gia, you need to leave. This is inappropriate and disrespectful. This is my home, a home I share with my husband. You can't just show up at my house like this." I shook my head. My voice had finally returned. Cory released her arm.

"You're just saying that cause he's standing there, but Kendra I can feel it in your touch, I know it by your kiss, you love me just as much as I love you." Gia wouldn't accept no and I knew that I had caused this.

Gia reached for me again, this time too swift for Cory's hands to catch her. Her fingers danced softly across my lips. The gentle caress of her hands somehow calmed me. I could hear him sigh behind me.

"Kendra Gia, I am so tired of this shit. You are trespassing. I'm not going to argue with you over my wife. She's just that, my wife. I got something for you though." Cory turned quickly and walked towards our room. I knew what it was about to do and it frightened me.

"Gia you need to leave right now." She looked at me. "Understand that this man is a quiet man but you have seen him when you push him. Leave." I pleaded with her.

"I'm not scared of him." She responded.

"You need to be, go Gia, we will talk about this later." I pushed her out the door. Cory's footsteps ricocheted throughout the house. I knew it wouldn't be long before he made his way back to front door. I was afraid he would come back with one of his guns.

"Promise you'll talk to me baby, promise." Gia spoke softly, then pressed her lips against mine. The softness of her lips pressed against mine, her MAC lipglosslip-gloss lingering on my lips. I pulled away from her and looked behind me just in time to see him turn the corner. I quickly closed the door and locked it.

"She's gone baby." I looked at Cory. "It's okay." I said.

"Kendra, it's not okay. It's not okay to watch you stammer and stutter over some woman. It's bad enough that you cheated on me with a woman, but then she won't go away. What the hell have you gotten us into?" I watched as flames of fury radiated from his body.

"We're not into anything baby it's over between her and I. It's over!" I said.

"It's over huh? If it's over can you tell me why you're standing in front of me wearing the same color lipstick your girl friend was wearing?" For a moment I couldn't breathe. I was afraid that if I so much as blinked, Cory's next move would be out the door.